"Riveting, thought-provoking ~~and inspiring~~ ....
that will take you on a vivid journey and leave you wanting more."
                    —Jennifer Salke, President, NBC Entertainment

A beautiful book of depth, humor, and vulnerability that asks the reader
to explore the most fundamental of questions: Am I truly living the life
I was meant to live? I dare you to make it to the last page unchanged.
                    —Luz Delgado, Editor and former Boston Globe journalist

"A beautiful self-discovery story that's so real it's hard to believe it's
fiction. You can't help but learn from these characters."
                    —Salaam Coleman Smith, Executive Vice President, ABC Family

So easy to be swept right into this story and to mourn the end of this
novel. A great fast read...and a story that will absolutely stay with you.
I can't wait for the sequel!
                    —Beverly Kaye, Bestselling Author of Love 'Em or Lose 'Em

Through vibrant prose and complex characters, Kohler takes us on a
journey into the inner lives of two admirable women, each searching for
elusive answers. Plot twists and turns makes this a riveting read that
will both entertain and make you think.
                    — Caroline Madden, Author, Marriage Family Therapist

Set aside an afternoon, make a pot of tea and curl up with this gripping
story that you'll read in one sitting! Like bread crumbs left along a path
in the forest to find your way home, Dawn Kohler speaks profound
truths through her characters that will stay with you long after the last
page is turned.
                    — Reagan Forlenzo, HR Consultant

The Invitation

A WEEKEND WITH EMMA

Dawn Kohler

BALBOA.
PRESS

A DIVISION OF HAY HOUSE

Balboa Press books may be ordered through booksellers or by contacting:

Balboa Press
A Division of Hay House
1663 Liberty Drive
Bloomington, IN 47403
www.balboapress.com
1 (877) 407-4847

Printed in the United States of America.

ISBN: 978-1-4525-1573-1 (sc)
ISBN: 978-1-4525-1575-5 (hc)
ISBN: 978-1-4525-1574-8 (e)

Library of Congress Control Number: 2014909578

Balboa Press rev. date: 8/26/2014

To my children, writers group and dear friends
who continue to inspire my journey.

Chapter 1

ONE PIECE OF INFORMATION CAN change a life forever.

I pulled the invitation out of the gray cotton envelope and looked at the handwritten note from Emma Daines. The words were written in a bold cursive that slanted to the right and became slightly jagged at the curves, denoting the not-so-steady hand of an aging woman. I slid my fingers across the crease of the small note and tented the invitation on the nightstand.

Two weeks ago, when the invitation arrived, I was a senior reporter working at the *Journal*, a regional paper in Syracuse. Three days later, I was fired, or laid off—or maybe they called it downsizing. I still can't remember the exact words Steven used, only the smirk on his sagging face as he watched me sink into my worn leather chair.

Steven escorted me out of the building that morning. The shock of a sudden death still numbed my skin as I left my office with nothing more than a few family pictures and the invitation from Emma. I slid the note into my purse before walking out the door, hoping he would forget that I ever received it.

"What time's your flight tomorrow?" David asked as he sat up in bed, clicking through late-night shows while I folded a sweater to put in my suitcase.

"Seven. I thought I'd take a cab to the airport."

"That's okay, baby; I'll take you. I can be a little late to work."

I walked back into my small, overstuffed closet, feeling the same agitation I had for months. Even before I lost my job, I felt uneasy. There was a growing pull inside of me, causing an anxiety I was becoming desperate to calm.

I looked through my rack of outdated clothes. "What do you wear to visit a woman like Emma Daines?" I wondered aloud.

"I'm sure she's just like everybody else!" David yelled from the bedroom. "I wouldn't get too worked up about it."

I shook my head and pulled open a drawer. Emma Daines was not like everybody else—at least not to me. She was the woman every journalist wanted to interview. Her books on social change were brilliant, as were her negotiation skills that had aided in bringing down the Berlin Wall. Yet the story every editor had wanted for decades was the one she never spoke of—the story about Sarah, her four-year-old daughter who was found missing late one night from their Connecticut home. After months of ransom notes, Sarah's deceased body was found by Emma. The details of the story were considered classified. There were no public comments from the family. Emma refused every interview. The media hungered for the facts—how she died and who was to blame. I wondered how Emma survived it, how she handled such a tragic change in her life, and what wisdom she had at seventy-two in the wake of such a history.

I walked back into the bedroom, and David reached for my hand. "I think you've packed enough sweaters," he said with a smile that lit up his chocolate-brown eyes, one just a little lazier than the other. "It's not that cold in California." He clicked off the TV and pulled me onto his bare chest, holding me so tight my ribs began to bend. I slithered in his arms until he loosened his grip.

"I don't get it," I said as I stood up to finish packing my suitcase. "I have tried to call Emma Daines for years to arrange an interview, and she never once returned my calls. Now she's inviting me to her home for the weekend. It just doesn't add up."

"Maybe she wants to meet the person who wrote all those articles."

"Meet me? She hasn't even wanted to speak with me. Damn, what if I wrote something she didn't like?"

"I doubt that."

"Then what if she's inviting me to her home because she wants me to write something for the *Journal*? What if she finally wants to give somebody the story about her daughter?"

David shook his head and flattened out the pillow. "Don't even go there. She's not going to talk about that story. Stick to her books about social anthropology or whatever it is she writes about."

"What do I tell her about my job?"

"Tell her the truth."

"And risk her asking me to leave? I can't do that." I picked up the note from the nightstand. "The invitation came to the *Journal*. She obviously wants to meet with a reporter." My hands began to moisten. "If I could somehow get her to talk about Sarah—a story like that could land me a job at the *New Yorker* or the *Times*." I clutched the invitation. "God, I need that right now."

"It isn't the story you need."

"I need a job."

"Or you could marry me and stop worrying about it." He got up and helped me zip my luggage.

"I said I would as soon as things settle down."

"You've been saying that for seven years."

I lifted my suitcase, and he pulled it out of my hand. "That's too heavy for you," he said. "It takes two hands."

"I'm fine, David. I can carry it myself." I set the luggage at the foot of the bed, and we crawled into the sheets from our respective sides.

"Your dad wants to be at our wedding. You can't keep putting this off."

I pulled the white blanket around my shoulder and turned toward the wall. I didn't want to think of my father as anything but strong and immortal, my soothing voice of reason that was always there to call, have lunch with, or share some historical event that never ceased to fascinate me. He had been so evasive about his heart condition that it was difficult to tell how much time he had left. My mother didn't say much either. We all just watched him grow frailer each month, still playing golf but spending more time in the cart than on the greens.

David turned over and brought me back into his arms. "You know, there is probably a reason you lost your—"

"Don't say it, David. I'm so sick of hearing, 'There is a reason for everything.' I really need to work right now. I feel lost without my job."

"You still have me."

I leaned into his face and kissed him good night, thinking, *I wish that were enough, baby. I really wish that were enough.*

❧

Rain pelted the tarmac as the final passengers boarded the flight. I climbed over a young couple nibbling at each other's faces like they wanted to eat each other alive to take my seat by the window. The woman excused herself and her husband as newlyweds and then resumed the smacking of lips and groping of thighs. I settled in and buckled my seatbelt, listening to their moans wondering if I would ever feel that way about David, so in love with him that I wanted to breathe every inch of his air. On some level, I yearned for those feelings. On another, it looked to be completely suffocating.

I put on a pair of earphones to distract myself from the whispers and heavy breathing and thought about the cabin we rented in Maine. David had taken me there for my twenty-eighth birthday, just a few months after we were introduced by a mutual friend. We spent the days sitting on a warm porch, watching the ducks swim through the tall reeds, reading to each other from our various books, wondering out loud about the author's point of view. David would always make a comment about what would hold up in a court of law while I reveled in how much he knew and the subtle ways he would find to move his body closer to mine. At night, we made love in that clumsy way new lovers do, not quite sure how to satisfy ourselves or each other. Our relationship never changed much from that weekend. The conversation was stimulating; yet emotionally, there was always a limit. He wanted a plan, a commitment, a way he could keep me safe from the world the way my father did when I was a child. I wanted to find stories, meet people, and challenge the fears that kept me living in a radius that never seemed to extend more than fifty miles from the town where I was raised.

Over the years, our routines set in, and here I was, engaged but still not ready to commit to marriage. I shifted again in my seat. The heat from the couple fogged the plane window, and it was not long until my restlessness from sitting next to them grew to the point of intolerance.

"Excuse me," I said as I climbed over the seats. They never looked up from each other while I straddled their legs and lunged into the aisle. I headed toward the tail of the cabin.

A few aisles back, I caught the eye of a pale, baby-faced man sitting in a middle seat, his large head and shoulders spiking up from the row of passengers. He stared at me as his plump lips formed an oval that looked too small for his face. I slowed my pace. *How do I know him?*

"Miss, you need to take your seat," the stewardess said. "And please fasten your seatbelt securely. The captain is expecting heavy turbulence throughout the flight."

I moved to the final row and took an aisle seat next to a little girl with a shiny, cropped haircut, her ears covered by headphones plugged into a small piano keyboard. She looked up at me, her wide eyes waiting for a cue. I held a smile through several breaths until her lips rose to expose a row of incoming teeth towering over a missing one. She gave me a quick, impish wave of the hand to finish her greeting and then resumed her focus on the keyboard. Her eyes flitted from her note sheet to the keys and then back again—something I remember doing a million times at her age. I imagined she wanted to please her mother, play her favorite song for her birthday, or be the kid in the recital who made her parents proud.

After a bumpy lift-off, the plane and my nerves leveled out as we headed west to California. The face of the man in the middle seat was still on my mind. Was he one of David's friends? Did he work in the same firm? The little girl next to me leaned her head against the seat and nodded off to sleep. I sat back, took a deep breath, and pulled out my file on Emma.

The first article I printed was from 1973: a young, broad-shouldered Emma standing next to the single-engine plane she flew into the outskirts of Vietnam to rescue her husband and another pilot after they were reported missing in action toward the end of the war. The event made her a national hero, a position that was elevated by her reclusiveness from media circles that made her all the more alluring. Her husband, Jon, went on to become a US senator, and Emma, a German American, was appointed ambassador to Germany. The next article featured a photo of President Ronald Reagan handing Emma a piece of the Berlin Wall, a gesture of appreciation for her advocacy work to remove the barrier and open the border.

The remaining articles were reviews on her books, a retirement announcement as a professor of social anthropology from Stanford University, and an obituary on her husband, Jon. It cited his life achievements, their forty-year marriage, and his remaining loved ones: Emma and their two adopted sons. Sarah was mentioned only as the deceased child of Emma and Jon. My further research on Sarah came up with nothing more than a thumbnail sketch of data about her disappearance and death. Who took her, where she was found, and how she died were not available to the public.

The seatbelt sign chimed just before the plane hit another pocket of turbulence. The little girl's eyes shot open as the plane took a deep dip. She sat up in her seat, took off her headphones, and looked at me.

"I'm going to see my grandparents," she blurted with bulging eyes that screamed, *I'm scared; please talk to me.* "Are you going to see your family?"

"No, my family lives in Virginia," I said, pushing down the tone of my voice to help calm both of us. I closed the file and tucked it into the seat pocket in front of me along with a book and a bottle of water.

"What happened to your hand?" she asked, staring at my fingers the way kids do when they can't make sense of something. My thumb and index finger on my right hand were the only ones fully formed at birth. The others withered on the side like small buds that never took form, stemming from a thin arm that was a few inches shorter than the other.

"You mean this one?" I asked as I flexed my left hand.

"No, silly, the other one."

"Oh, this one. It was just the way I was born."

"Does it hurt?"

"No, it doesn't hurt," I said as I pinched my thumb and finger together.

"It kind of looks like a claw."

"Yeah, I used to get that a lot when I was your age. Kate the Claw, Crabby, and during Christmas, Jimmy Delany use to call me Santa Claw." She giggled as I reached out and pinched my fingers in the air.

"That's funny. Can you tie your shoes?"

"Yep."

"Can you ride a bike?"

"One of my favorite things to do."

"Can you climb a tree?"

"Nope. Not because of my hand, but because I'm afraid of heights. Looking down from high places makes me feel nervous and sweaty all over."

"Like being in a plane high up in the sky?"

"Planes are not too bad as long as I don't look out the window. But climbing trees or standing on tall buildings is really scary."

7

She nodded her head. "So is the big drop ride at the fair!"

"Yeah, that would be frightening. I'd rather eat ice cream at the fair."

"Me too," she said as she looked down at my hand. "Can you pick up a pencil?"

"I sure can. I'm even a writer. I pick up pencils for a living."

My eyes shot up. That's how I know that guy. He was from the *Journal*. The intern they brought in last year, the kid who became a reporter just before they laid off the senior staff. My heart began to race. Were they sending him to meet with Emma?

"Do you write books?" I felt a tug on my sleeve. "Do you write books for kids like me? I read a lot of books. My favorite is *Amelia Bedelia*. I don't like books about vampires or spiders. I only like chapter books, and my teacher gave me a ribbon last year 'cause I read more books than anybody else in the class for the whole year. Can you believe it? The whole year."

"Wow, I bet that is a lot of books," I said, looking down the aisle, trying to remember what row he was in. Steven knew I had received the invitation. He assumed Emma Daines was looking for regional publicity for a book and didn't show much interest. With all the commotion around the layoffs, I thought he would have forgotten about it. I stared at the back of the intern's large head. But what if he didn't forget? What if they contacted Emma and were sending this guy instead?

I flashed back to the day I was fired. The sneer of revenge on Steven's face and the feeling of blood draining out of my body as events earlier that month snapped together like the sharp end of a whip. I'm sure I made the layoff list when I turned down the assignment he gave me to cover the Nelson twins at the race track and sent in an article on a medical student who lost funding due to budget cuts instead. After fifteen years at the *Journal*, I was hungrier than ever for stories that had substance. Steven was hungry for hits and clicks on the website.

My mouth soured as I looked at the back of the intern's head. This was my chance at a real story, a national interest piece, a story with meaning that would hopefully bring insight into how to manage the challenges we face in our life. I couldn't let that intern take this from me.

"Do you want to draw?" the little girl asked. "I brought lots of paper and colored pencils. They're new. My brother hasn't even played with them yet."

I stared down the aisle. The seatbelt light flashed again, along with the ring of the intercom. "Passengers, we are sorry about the turbulence. The flight crew does expect it to be bumpy through the remainder of the flight, so please remain in your seats with your seatbelts securely fastened."

The flight attendant strapped herself into the wall seat in the rear, staring down the aisle like a hall monitor. My legs tightened. I released a deep breath and looked at the little girl, her eyes pleading for a playmate. "Yeah," I said. "Let's draw."

The plane took a deep bank turn into the fog, and we started our final descent into the San Francisco airport. My chest tightened as I waited for the landing, hoping to get on the ground safely while I wondered what I was going to say when I caught up to the guy from the *Journal*. He was at least ten rows ahead. I would have to catch him on the ramp.

The plane hung in the gray mist. Seconds ticked away as if time had stopped until I felt a bump and the yellow lines of the runway appeared. The little girl packed up her keyboard, and the attendant approached to escort her to the front of the plane.

The man from the *Journal* popped out from the crowd as passengers grabbed their overhead luggage and lined up, facing the door. I rummaged through my mind, trying to remember his name, wondering if I ever knew it. I was so driven to make a name for myself as a writer that I didn't pay much attention to the interns—or anybody else, for that matter.

I felt the little girl reach for my hand, her warm fingers wrapping around my stunted ones as a sudden flush of embarrassment melted into an unfamiliar comfort.

"Do you want to meet my grandparents?" she asked while we waited in line for the forward passengers to depart.

"I would love to meet them. But I'm afraid I'm going to have to run as soon as we get off the plane."

Her eyes looked down and her hand remained snug in mine until we exited the door. I bent down to say goodbye.

"Have fun with your grandparents this weekend."

"Just a second," she said as she fumbled through her pink backpack, pulling out her pencils and papers and setting them on the floor next to her. I looked through the legs of the crowd, trying to keep track of him. My temples pulsed with the clenching of my jaw.

"I want to give you something." She opened her drawing pad and handed me a picture of a long, auburn-haired girl with curls flowing down her back, climbing a tall tree.

"It's a picture of you," she said. "See, you're not afraid to climb the tree."

I smiled through tense skin. The warm glow in my chest I felt from her picture was quickly overpowered by the fear that I would lose the intern from the *Journal* if I stood there one more second.

"Thank you," I said as I helped her pack up her pencils. "I wish I was your age and we could go climb trees together." I looked up the ramp. There was no sight of him.

"I'm so sorry; I have to run to catch up with somebody. I hope you have a really special weekend with your family." I resisted the urge to hug her, then extended the handle of my carry-on and took off running.

The airport was a dense sea of hurried people all moving in different directions. I scanned the crowd, looking for his head. Cafés, stores, and restrooms lined the corridor. *God, he could be anywhere.* My gut kept telling me to move toward the door, an instinct I had learned to trust as a journalist. I stepped onto the escalator headed down to baggage claim when I saw the back of his head walking out the exit.

"Excuse me." I picked up my luggage and carried it over my head, walking down the escalator until I was stopped by a large man who was impossible to pass. The steps melted under the floor one by one until the man in front of me departed and I took off at a runner's pace. By the time I reached the exit, the intern was stepping into a cab that was out of yelling distance. I ran toward the closest taxi while his cab pulled away from the curb.

"Where you going, miss?" asked the driver.

"Just follow that cab in front of us," I said as I caught my breath. "We are going to the same place."

Chapter 2

WE FOLLOWED THE CAB THROUGH the rainy city to a steel and glass hotel with a circular driveway. Cars and cabs vibrating with impatience moved one by one to the door of the lobby. The guy from the *Journal* jumped out of his cab. I paid mine, grabbed my bag, and started heading for the door. *He's probably here to visit friends,* I thought, *and I'm just being ridiculous. Still, I can't take the chance that he'll show up at Emma's.* My pace quickened as I passed the two men in front of me and slid in the registry line behind him. *Think. What is his name again?* I tipped over my luggage to get his attention. He turned, looked at the bag on the floor, and then met my eyes with a glare.

"Oh, hi," I said, lifting the handle of the carry-on off the ground. "I know you."

"Mike," he said. "We used to work together."

"Oh, yes, Mike. You were the intern at the *Journal.* You wrote some great stuff."

"I doubt you ever read my stuff," he said under his breath.

"So what brings you to San Francisco? Are you covering a story?"

"Just here for the night. I'm going to some place by Carmel in the morning."

"Aptos?"

"Yeah, that's the place." His shoulders let down. "Emma Daines wants to talk to a reporter. You know that old lady that saved her husband from that prison camp in Vietnam?"

I cringed at his description and the thought of him interviewing her for anything. "Really? Then it's a good thing I ran into you. Did Steven tell you that the invitation to meet with her was addressed to me?"

"No. He just said she wanted to meet with somebody from the *Journal*."

"Well, I think there has been a mistake," I said, setting back my shoulders. "I just took a job with the *New York Times*, and we are covering the story. Emma Daines has been notified, and she is expecting me at 5:00 p.m. today."

"You're kidding. Does Steven know this?"

"I'm not sure. But it might be embarrassing if we both showed up, don't you think?"

He stared over the lobby crowd, squinting his eyes and shaking his head. "I knew this was a lame assignment, if it's an assignment at all. Emma Daines hates journalists."

"How do you know?"

"Are you kidding? During Vietnam, when she was hot news, she told a journalist from the *Times* she would give him a personal interview. She sent him to a hotel in Hanoi to meet her and never showed up." He grunted. "That guy got famous, though."

I remembered reading about the incident. The hotel she sent him to was a cover for a dilapidated prison holding mentally ill American soldiers. He did get a story that ended up freeing the men. But he never met Emma Daines.

"I have a fraternity brother that lives in the city. I'd rather spend the weekend with him anyway," he said, twisting his finger into his ear. "But I don't know. I better call Steven."

"You do that. And let Steven know I'm covering the story."

I pulled out of line acting far more confident than I was, praying under my breath that I wouldn't run into him again or hear from

Steven. The concierge gave me a map and pointed me toward the rental car desk. I was one step closer to meeting Emma Daines, a thought that brought on a wave of trepidation. She was expecting to meet a reporter, and I was feeling raw and exposed without my job, like traveling without clothes on my body. I shook off my angst, opened the map, and focused on the next leg of my journey—driving in pea soup fog to a beach town over fifty miles away.

The fog cleared as I made my way south, and Aptos was much easier to find than I had imagined. Just past Santa Cruz, I exited west and meandered along a redwood-lined street into the small beachside village of quaint shops, art studios, and an old, rustic train station that gave the town a nineteenth-century feel. I stopped at a small store. The entrance was framed with fresh flowers tiered in white vases under a green awning with rope fringe that danced in the light wind. I turned off the car and called David. He planned to leave work early to play golf with my dad. The two of them were probably just teeing off, talking about how great it would be if David and I could join the club as a married couple, speculating about my reluctance like two boys trying to figure out crop circles. His voice mail picked up.

"Hey, David. I'm here, and all is well. I'll check in with you later."

The array of brightly colored flowers made me feel more alive. I picked up a bouquet of white tulips and walked into the store. An elderly man greeted me from behind the register, and an older woman in a long knit purple sweater and knee-high black boots was browsing the greeting cards on a nearby stand. I pulled out the invitation from Emma.

"Excuse me," I said, showing the man the card, "do you know where the Tea House is? There is no address. It just says Sea Cliff Drive."

"Ah, you're going to Emma Daines's house," he replied. The woman looked up from the greeting cards. Our eyes met, and we exchanged a smile. Her face was round, with full lips, soft features, and light-blue eyes that were set off by brown skin and thick, gray-white hair, cropped like a cresting wave just beneath her chin. I found myself captivated by her natural beauty and warm presence.

"You turn left at the light," he said, pointing outside. "Go to the top of the hill, and make another left at the fork. About half a mile down on the right, you will see a big red mailbox. Make a right, and you'll find her place at the end of the dirt road."

"Sunflowers," the woman said as she walked toward me, staring at my tulips. "Emma loves big yellow sunflowers."

"We have some out front," the man said. "Would you like me to get them for you?"

"Yes. Thank you." I looked at the woman as she smiled back at me. "Are you a friend of Emma's?"

"You could say that. You must be Kate, the reporter from Syracuse."

Great, she is telling her friends I work at the Journal. "Yes, that would be me," I said through a forced grin.

"If you are looking for the perfect gift for Emma, get the flowers, then go across the street to the open air stand and buy her some fresh mint leaves. She loves to make tea concoctions with mint leaves."

"Thank you. I'm sorry, but I didn't get your name."

She reached out her left hand to shake mine. I was bewildered but relieved. Most people shake with their right hand, which was awkward for me. I usually slid my dwarf fingers in my pocket and offered up my left. I feared that made me look lazy or inconsiderate. But I'd rather risk that perception than greet somebody with a deformity that might make them feel uncomfortable.

"I'm Camille," she said. Her touch was firm and gentle. In her voice was a hint of a Latin accent. "Do you mind if I give you one more piece of advice about Emma?"

"Please."

"I realize you are a journalist, and I'm sure you are eager to get to know Emma, but do yourself a favor, and don't ask her about her daughter. Some things are best left alone."

"That will be $12.72," the man said as he rang up the flowers.

Camille locked on to my eyes, raising her brow as if she were waiting for some sign that I would honor her request.

I rifled through my purse to find the exact change. By the time I had finished my purchase, Camille was gone. I looked out the window and watched her cross the street.

"Who was that woman?" I asked the clerk.

"One of the locals around here. Nice lady."

I looked back out the window. Did she really know Emma that well? Were they friends? Or was she the town gossip, trying to protect the local celebrities? The warning to not ask about Sarah left me with an eerie feeling. What could have happened to her that couldn't be talked about? I thanked the clerk and walked out to the car.

Rays of warm sunlight pierced through the redwood trees as I swerved around the bend to the unmarked red mailbox with the rusty brown flag. I slowed the car. A flash of heat rose in my face, and my fingers began to tremble. Did I prepare the right questions? Had I done enough research? Was I wearing the right outfit? I turned onto the gravel road, my hands vibrating on the wheel as I drove to the end of a turnabout that circled a large magnolia tree. Two dogs ran down the steps of a redwood deck that extended from the white ranch style home. A yellow lab barked an uncommitted warning while a smaller brown and gray mutt wagged his tail and jumped up and down beside the car. I took a few deep breaths and turned off the engine. The sprawling, understated home seemed to fit my image of Emma. The tranquil surrounding eased my tension.

I stepped out of the car. The yellow lab lumbered up to me and smelled my hand while the other dog danced on its hind legs.

"Hey, little dog. You sure are cute."

The house was quiet with an open feel. A soft breeze came up from the ocean, lightly ringing the pewter wind chimes that hung from the eaves. My chest tingled as I stepped up to the porch, where a book lay open on the deep seat of a white cushioned chair.

"Hello!" I shouted through the Dutch door entrance that was half open, like a European bakery. "Anybody home?"

The lab sat staring at me with its tongue out. The little dog just kept yapping until I noticed the note taped under the doorbell.

Kate,

I had to run out for a moment. Make yourself at home. Your room is the first cottage on the left just outside the kitchen door. Sadie and Max will show you the way.

The strain in my forehead continued to ease as the casual tone of her note helped release another layer of tension. I looked down at the lab. "Are you Sadie or Max?" The dogs ran through the door in front of me, racing across the used brick entryway and down the hall toward the kitchen. My eyes opened wide. To the right of the entry was a spacious living room with floor-to-ceiling bookshelves that wrapped around the walls, edging up to a river rock fireplace that rose through the top of the white wooden beam ceiling. The smell of freshly watered plants mixed with the musky scent of old books took me like an aphrodisiac. The energy coming off the books spines was palpable.

I meandered down the hall, where rows of family pictures hung in old rustic frames. There were several photos of Emma camping, fishing, and riding horses with two boys of Asian descent. I assumed they were the children she adopted after the death of her daughter. The little boys were smiling or laughing in each photo. The pictures were so candid that they were comforting.

Hanging in the middle of the wall was a wedding picture in which a young, full-lipped Emma stood dutifully next to her red-haired husband in a decorated navy uniform. He was more handsome, or perhaps more proud, than in other pictures I had seen. Below was a black and white portrait of Emma holding a curly-haired baby girl. She looked down on the child with a loving gaze; the baby's small bare feet rose from a blanket as she played with a locket held by a thin chain around Emma's neck. I let out an audible sigh. *Sarah.* I stepped closer to the picture. There were only a few public photos of Sarah, and all were from a distance. Seeing her up close made her seem so real—and Emma so human. I felt my chest expand. This was not just a story; it was the life of a child.

As I moved down to the end of the hall, there was a picture of Emma with her arm around a woman who could have been her sister. Both were dressed in hiking gear, and the backdrop appeared to be the sheer rocks jutting up from the floor of the Yosemite Valley. Below was a photo of her standing next to an open cockpit airplane with Anne and Charles Lindbergh. The photo stood alone as the only picture of Emma that noted her public status.

My phone vibrated, startling me into the moment. I pulled it out of my pocket to see a reminder on my calendar about a cocktail party sponsored by the *Journal*. My small fingers curled into my hand, and nails dug into my skin. I tucked the phone in the bottom of my leather bag and peeked down the hall to the bedrooms. I took a step toward the rooms and then stepped back. I wondered if she lived alone or if she had a companion she somehow kept from the press. The hall emptied to a large kitchen, where several bouquets of dying leaves were strung upside down from pot holders hung from low beams that ran up the tilted ceiling. I suddenly remembered what the woman in the store said about the mint leaves. *Damn.* I wished I would have picked some up. I took another step.

Squeeel … uf … squeal. I jumped back, holding my chest. The blue dog toy I stepped on was inflating in front of me while my heart was racing its way back to New York. I took a few deep breaths and walked around the kitchen. A set of bowls was in the sink, and a flame was burning on high next to a teapot on the gas stove. I turned off the stove and felt the teapot next to it. It was still warm. The thought of her being gone longer excited me. I was enjoying the sense of intimacy that came with being alone in her home, like I was getting to know her without the pretense that conversation can bring.

Across the room, the late afternoon sun was beaming in from a greenhouse window that cast a shaft of light into a small alcove off the side of the kitchen. On the narrow wall to the alcove was a needlepoint saying hanging in a frame.

Change Happens to Everyone
Wisdom Occurs when You Use the Change Wisely

That's worth writing down, I thought as I peered into the room to see an antique roll-top desk and a small wooden chair. I stepped into the small office to grab a pen when the *Journal's* blue logo caught my eye. On top of the desk was a stack of paper clippings. My heart deepened its beat as I thumbed through articles that I had written over the past several years. At the bottom of the stack was a white envelope with my name typed on a label in the top right-hand corner. The envelope was sealed. I held it up to the light, faintly seeing a document through the cover. The back door rattled open. I tossed down the envelope and straightened the papers on the desk.

"Down; down, Sadie," said a man.

I slid sideways out of the alcove and back into the kitchen.

"Oh. Hello," he said, taking a step back. "You must either be the reporter from New York or a very well-dressed prowler."

"Hi, I'm Kate." I put my hands in my pockets so he wouldn't see them shaking.

"I'm Brian. We spoke a few weeks ago."

"Oh, yes. Thank you for helping arrange the date. I'm so glad this weekend worked out for her. I know she has a busy schedule."

"When Emma wants to meet somebody, she makes the time." He whirled around the kitchen, putting a coffee cup in the sink and a file on the counter.

"Your cottage is out back," he said, pointing into the yard. "The one next to the worldwide headquarters of Emma Daines."

I looked out the window to see two small A-framed cottages at the end of the brick patio.

"When Emma gets back, could you tell her that her schedule is here on the counter, and her speaking engagement in Europe next month was canceled due to travel warnings? She'll want to go anyway, so good luck when she gets that news."

"Do you know when you expect her back?"

"She should be here any minute, so you might not have any more time to snoop around the house."

"I wasn't snooping."

"You reporters call it whatever you like," he said as he grabbed an apple off the counter and walked down the hall to the front door. "Tell Emma I'll see her on Monday."

I waited until I heard him drive away, walked back to the alcove, and picked up the large white envelope. *What could be in here?* I held it back to the light while the dogs began to whine at the back door and the sound of a woman singing carried through the open window.

I slid the envelope back under the articles and rushed to the door to let out the dogs.

Sadie and Max barreled toward the woman while I stood in the doorway, holding my breath.

"You are such good doggies," the woman said, patting the round chest of the yellow lab. Emma looked up and took several long strides toward me. "You must be Kate. It's so good to meet you."

Our eyes met in a soft gaze. I felt my face blush as a smile rose without effort. Emma looked older than I had imagined. The left side of her face drooped slightly, and the corner of her mouth fell like an apostrophe. Her long gray hair was pulled back in a loose ponytail, softening her angular nose and large, deep-set green eyes. Her sturdy frame stood tall as she greeted me with both hands, one firmly shaking my left while the other gently cupped our grip.

"I'm so glad you could make it," she said as she squeezed my hand.

"I wouldn't have missed an opportunity to meet you," I said in a high-pitched voice that didn't sound like my own. I suddenly felt overdressed standing next to her in my gray wool business suit and she in her denim button-down gardening shirt, leggings, and a pair of winter Ugg boots. "Oh ... one of the stove burners was on when I walked through the kitchen. Hope you don't mind that I turned it off."

Emma rolled her eyes upward, and the left side of her face pleated into soft wrinkles. "That explains why my insurance went up when I hit seventy-two. They must figure in the next five years, I'm either going to die or burn something down." She looked at me and winked. "I think I'd rather burn something down."

I laughed, not anticipating her charm.

"How was your flight?"

"It was good," I said as I reached down and patted the yellow lab. "What a beautiful place to live."

"Yes, I feel very fortunate. I do love it here," she said as she picked up the little dog and cradled her to her chest. "Have you seen your room yet?"

"No, I just got here."

"Good. Let's grab your luggage and get you settled in."

The yellow lab followed us out to the car, and I noticed my nerves and trembling hands had settled down. I pulled my carry-on from the trunk and followed Emma around the side yard through a lattice archway covered with overgrown vines that gave birth to deep-purple flowers. The path led back to the open courtyard off the kitchen which was bordered by a redwood forest. Two small cottage-style bungalows edged the property, staged between large redwood trees. A stream ran through the west side of the property, paralleling a dirt trail that led down the hill. I took a deep breath of the fresh, clean air and began to feel at ease.

We walked toward the cottage closest to the stream. The purple flowering vines ran up the side of the A-frame room, outlining the roof like holiday trimming.

"I think you'll like it here," she said, lifting the red nylon keychain from around the doorknob and inserting it into the old, rusty lock.

Her knuckles were large and bony but seemed to move with ease as she patiently inserted the key and turned it several times to open the door. "Here you are. I call this the Sunrise Room. It's one of my favorite places to write."

Emma walked across the old wooden floor and pulled open the handmade drapes to a large window that looked over the stream, southwest toward the ocean. The horizon was barely distinguishable through the gray fog that was rolling up the coastline.

"I can see why you like to write here," I said, feeling the peaceful energy that defined the room.

"It has good light. And I love a room with good light."

I set my jacket on the full-size bed that was covered with a red-and-tan quilt. A white wooden nightstand was next to the mattress, and a few feet away was a doorway to a small half-bath with a standalone basin. The side wall was covered with an antique writer's desk with shelves of old books above. The other corner had a potbelly stove vented by a black pipe that ran through the top of the roof.

"I think you will find everything you need here," Emma said with a smile.

I looked around for a plug for my computer. There wasn't a phone jack, a cable cord, or even a clock. I suddenly felt a bit foolish, standing there with a bag that was weighed down by my laptop, a blow dryer, and enough office tools to blow the circuit on her house.

"Make yourself comfortable. And don't worry if you see a raccoon or two walking across the window sill. Those two down there like to peek in on the guests."

I followed the point of her long finger to the raccoons jumping across a rock. "We have raccoons at home. They won't bother me," I said, looking out the window and then back at Emma. "Can I do anything for you while I'm here? Help with dinner or pick up some groceries?"

"No, no; just relax and enjoy yourself. When guests come in from the city, they always need a little time to unwind. I thought we would walk down into town in about an hour to get some dinner."

"That sounds wonderful."

She smiled in an almost childlike way, handing me the key and closing the door behind her.

I walked over to the window and peered down to the trickling stream. The raccoons were playing by the water. The larger of the two was perched on a rock with his bushy tail cocked in the air. He waited, still, and then leaped across the river, grabbing the tail of the other and then running away. The smaller one waited for his return, as if not caring too much about the outcome. *Ahh … I should try again to reach David.* I pulled out my cell phone and tapped his number. The line was silent. The cottage was out of range for service. My throat tightened when I realized that also meant I wouldn't be able to receive e-mail. I recalled Emma's words. *You have all that you need here.* I was starting to realize that "need" was a relative term.

I slipped off my shoes and fell face-up onto the bed, my body sinking deep into the mattress while my mind continued to race. I took a few deep breaths to try to slow myself down, and in minutes, I was again aware of the anxiety that rose just under my thoughts. It was like living with gravel in my shoes, a constant irritation bubbling above the insistent pulled of an undertow.

I lay awake on the bed for a few minutes and then got up and looked through the shelves above the writing desk. There were rows of thick books on ancient civilizations woven among hardback classics and a few modern novels. I scanned up the shelf, looking for something to read, when the low buzz of an insect caught my attention. It stopped and then started again. I stepped back, and the sound got louder as a honey bee flew off the top shelf and circled the room. It landed on the drape and began to crawl up the cloth, inching its way toward the edge. I took a breath, and it stopped, as if it knew I was watching.

I looked around the room for something to help me guide it out the window when it flew off again toward the ceiling, banked before hitting the wall, and mounting with speed, headed straight toward my face. It jetted through the long strands of my hair while I ducked, and then it landed on the cloth cover of a large book sitting on the top shelf. My dad kept bees and jarred honey for a hobby, so they never bothered me, but I wasn't interested in having it for a roommate for the weekend. I opened the window, grabbed a cup on the basin, and moved toward the shelf. The bee was out of reach.

I looked around the room for something to use as a ladder and decided the armless cloth chair next to the desk would give me the right lift. Standing on the sagging cushion, I slowly moved toward the bee. When I got within inches, I took a swift punch and captured it in the cup. *My dad would be proud,* I thought as I slid the book toward me, keeping the bee in place. I put my ear up to the cup. Waiting for the sound of a buzz, I heard the ripping noise of cloth as my foot tore through the seat of the chair. The book tilted off the shelf, hitting me in the chest as I tumbled onto the floor, and the bee shot out the window. I lay there for a moment and then rolled up on my knees. The chair looked like a small bomb had gone off in the seat. Cotton and springs were exposed—beyond anything I could pretend to repair. I looked around the room, cringing at the look of the chair until another sight caught my eye. The book that hit me was actually a box concealed as an old dictionary. Inside was a stack of papers held together by a black spiral binder. I picked it up, turned it over, and read the cover:

Summons to the Soul
A Memoir
by Emma Daines

Her memoir? Was she intending to publish this? I looked up at the empty space on the top shelf. Was this hidden for somebody to find later? I opened the cover and read an acknowledgment: *To Camille, with deep love and appreciation.*

Camille? The woman in the store who I thought was the town gossip? I stood and looked out the window toward the house. There was no sign of Emma. My mouth watered, my chest swelling with a desire to open the next page, abated by the churning sense of guilt I would feel for reading something so personal that it was hidden. I put the memoir back in the box, ran my fingers through my hair, and then picked it up again. It was the box the bee landed on. *My dad loves bees. Maybe this was a sign that I'm supposed to read it. Oh my God; I'm starting to sound like David.* I jumped up and returned the empty box to its position on the bookshelf, moved the ripped chair under the desk, and stared at the memoir. Maybe Emma wanted me to find it. Maybe that's why she put me in this room. The justification was a mild sedative to my guilt—enough to make me decide to read the first few pages. I pulled out a file from my briefcase. Using the folder as a cover, I gazed over a brief introduction and began to read.

> I watched my mother take her last breath the day after my twelfth birthday. One cannot fathom the true void of such a loving source, nor can one tolerate the abject pain of emptiness as she left the body that once incubated me into being. A nurse spoke to me about feelings of loss; yet her words were as empty as the shock that my mother was gone—that I could not touch her face, nor could she touch mine. *Loss,* a word, simply does not give justice to what this does to the inner core of a child. When safety is shattered, survival is compromised, and the heart is broken and bleeding without the feminine wings of comfort available to bring me back to my core. It was like living without oxygen. The world that was once exciting, untainted, and filled with adventures to one's soul had moved to a black and white realm of pictures that felt detached from reality. I no longer knew who I was. The first major transition in my life had begun.

Her words took my breath away. Her prose touched me in a place that made me feel her pain, or somehow my own. I sat up and pushed back my shoulders, wanting to be alert for every word.

> I was summoned to adulthood not only by the events of that twelfth year, but also by a father who chose to replace his wife with me. This was not unusual at the time, nor in East Germany, where few words were spoken and the black veil of oppression grew more ominous each year. When my mother passed, there were no more visitors. I was now my father's possession. In one vein, this was frightening to me, in the other, it was an odd delight. It was the first time in my young life when any man, including my father, had given me attention; only to be followed by the shame of his avoidance and the feeling of deep inadequacy that became so insidious it soon defined me.
>
> Loss, as I would learn at such a young age, involves some form of grief, some form of resistance, and some form of exposure. The exposure to self and to others is like the yolk broken open from an egg. In delicate times such as these, we are left vulnerable to ourselves and to the world that surrounds us.
>
> Thus begin the patterns of our lives and the barriers to the essence of our souls—internal walls crafted by the budding beliefs of who we are, designed to protect that which feels too fragile and undesirable to expose. By the age of thirteen, a growing ambition suppressed the longing for my mother and my need to be cared for by a safe and trusted other. I was an adult, and the world became a place to prove myself worthy.

Chapter 3

THE KITCHEN DOOR FLUNG OPEN. Emma called for the dogs, and the clicking of pellets hitting an empty bowl carried through the open window in my cottage. I closed the manuscript and slid it under the quilt. The guilty feelings had abated and were replaced with a sense of sadness, and connection. I had never had Emma's experiences, but how she experienced them was hitting a chord deep inside of me. Her memoir was so real and raw that it left me feeling exposed.

I rummaged through my luggage, pulled out a heavy sweater, and then hurried out the door to meet Emma for dinner.

"Are you hungry?" she asked as she grabbed a walking stick.

"I'm getting there."

"Good. Let's go get something delicious." She began singing what sounded like an improvisational song about the raccoons and started marching down the hill in her ankle-high boots and a dark-blue coat that waved open as she moved.

Halfway down the trail, Emma stopped at a lookout spot shaded by a redwood that seemed to be growing upward from the cliff, its large roots exposed and entangled like snarled ropes growing up from the ground. Emma looked at the tree. "Have you ever seen a tree like this, Kate?"

"No, I can't say I have."

"See those exposed tap roots, tangled together, fighting to secure themselves to the earth? They are all climbing over one another to find the best vantage point." She hit an exposed root ball with her walking stick. "Half these roots are strangling the other half. All out for themselves, as if they don't even know that they are all part of the same damn tree. Ridiculous, isn't it?"

"Why do you think it grows like that?"

"Survival. The first order of life is always survival. If you can't survive, nothing else really matters, now, does it?"

"Well, then, maybe the roots aren't being ridiculous."

She started to laugh. "Maybe. Maybe. What do you feel like for dinner?" she asked as she resumed her march down the hill.

We followed the well-worn trail bordered by mounds of wild grass and flowering yellow weeds. The path led to a backstreet that opened to the small village. The people we passed were walking dogs or riding bikes, and each waved or said hello to Emma. She returned the greeting with a wide smile, addressing every person and dog by name, never once slowing the pace of her cadence as we made our way toward the end of town. Just past the flower shop, we crossed over a worn street and slipped into a small bistro with an Italian flair. Emma waved to a young man behind the bar where a group of people were gathered around a small TV.

"This is one of my favorite places," she said, taking a corner booth that I imagined was somehow hers. "They have great salads and even better pizzas."

I opened the menu, trying to focus on the selection while my mind raced with questions. *Why am I here? What does Emma want from me? What kind of pizza should I eat? What if Mike calls the* Journal *and they send him down to interview Emma in the morning?*

"Order whatever you want," Emma said, pulling up her eyeglasses from a brushed silver chain she wore around her neck.

What I wanted was a thick-crust pizza with sausage, pepperoni, and extra cheese, but this was California, so I thought I better order something with a vegetable on it.

"Would you ladies like some water?" asked the waitress.

"We would love some. And I imagine Kate here is getting pretty hungry by now, so we might want to order."

I glanced down the menu. "I think I will have the basil and tomato pizza."

"Then let's get two pizzas," Emma said. "I'm going to have the pepperoni and sausage."

Damn! I don't even like basil. The waitress picked up our menus and left while Emma took off her glasses and started to wipe the lens with a small white tissue. "Thank you for coming all the way to Aptos. I was so looking forward to meeting you."

"My pleasure. I've read your books, written reviews, and followed your career since you were an ambassador. I couldn't wait to finally meet you in person."

Emma's eyes rolled up and around, her high cheeks flushing with a blush. Then, I could hear myself starting to ramble the way I did when I got around certain people, like my English Lit professor, who vacationed with Hemingway, or my mother when she flew in from business trips. I forced myself to stop and then anguished through a moment of silence.

"Do you come here often?" I asked.

"A few times a week. It's nice to stroll down for dinner."

"Do you walk up that same trail at night?"

"Usually. It helps me digest the pizza."

I nodded. My toes began fidgeting in my shoes while my small fingers crawled into my hand.

"So tell me about you. How long have you been with the *Journal?*"

"Oh … about fifteen years."

"You don't look old enough to have been working for fifteen years."

"I took an internship there during college, and the years seemed to fly by after that."

"They do fly by." Emma gazed down at my hand while I rubbed my thumb and finger across the seam of the white cloth napkin. "Does Ed Caprice still work there?"

My eyes darted toward the bar as my stomach tensed. "No. He passed away last year. How did you know Ed?"

"Oh, I'm sorry to hear that. He was a friend of mine from college. We lost touch about ten years ago." She shook her head. "That's too bad he is no longer with us."

I moved the cloth napkin from the table to my lap. "Sounds like you are familiar with the *Journal*."

"No, not really. Although it does interest me."

I started to smell the need for publicity. The *Journal* had the best reach for authors in the region. If she wanted to promote a book, I would be of little use to Emma. "I must admit," I said, "I was surprised to receive your invitation. I wasn't sure if you were looking for me or a journalist from the *Journal*."

"Both," she said as the lines around her eyes folded into soft pleats. "I was looking for a publication that had a certain demographic, and I wanted to meet you, too. I guess I just got lucky."

I forced a smile, as my thumb and finger rubbed together like cricket legs between the cloth linen. We sat through an awkward pause before a barrel-chested man in a red bar apron dropped off a warm basket of bread. "Have you ladies seen the news?" he said as he looked at Emma. "There was a big earthquake down south."

"No, I haven't," she said as she extended her neck toward the TV behind the bar. "Where down south?"

"It looks like the epicenter was right on the border between San Diego and Mexico. You're not traveling down there this week, are you?"

"No, I don't think so." Emma stared off toward the TV as the waitress approached our table. "Has Camille been in tonight?"

"I haven't seen her."

Emma reached in her purse and pulled out her cell phone. "Three missed calls," she said under her breath. "I'm sorry, Kate, but we need to check on something." She picked up her jacket and asked the waitress to deliver our pizzas next door. I followed her hurried pace as she led me out through a narrow cobblestone walkway to a small art studio with a window that faced the street. She pulled open the door. A bell chimed, and the smell of oil paints carried us into the room. On the walls hung framed pictures of flower fields, rolling vineyards, and small stucco churches perched over abandoned, windy beaches. We walked across the wood floors to the corner of the studio, where a woman was sitting on a small stool, painting a bouquet of brightly colored flowers rising from a deformed mustard vase. I recognized her from the flower store. Her thick gray hair was layered to the collar of her long lavender-blue sweater. Emma walked up to her and brushed her hand down Camille's arm. "I'm sorry I just saw your calls."

"Did you see the news?" she asked.

"We just heard about it. Have you heard from Jess?"

"No," she said, dabbing her brush in the paint like she was trying to shake the nerves out of her hand. "Cell coverage is out from San Diego to Ensenada. We've lost contact with the girl's family, too."

"I'm sure they are both fine," Emma said, rubbing her shoulders. "Oh, I'm sorry, Camille. This is—"

"Kate," Camille said as she turned toward me. "We met earlier today at the market." Camille's eyes locked softly onto mine, reminding me of her advice to not ask Emma about her daughter. She dipped her brush in thinner and wiped it clean with a white tattered cloth.

"Let me show you what we're talking about," Camille said as she rose from her chair and walked us to the back of the art studio. She opened a door at the end of a short hall to an office. Around the room was a long, L-shaped desk with several computer monitors and a small conference table in the middle that sat on a sisal rug. In front of one of the computers was a young man with matted blonde hair pecking away on a keyboard, barely acknowledging that we had entered. Camille and Emma looked over his shoulder at the recent newsfeeds while I studied the room. The walls were covered with neatly lined pictures of grade school children and a world map with red dots throughout the hemispheres.

"Please keep trying to reach Jess," she said to the young man. She moved toward the center of the office and explained that we had just entered the control room of Oasis, a nonprofit organization that she had started more than forty years ago. The organization raised money through private donations and used the funds to adopt and educate children targeted for slavery and prostitution.

"How do you find the children?" I asked.

"Through our community partners. They know the tactics of the sex traffickers and let us know what children are about to be sold."

"What kind of tactics do they use?"

"It varies. Some go into villages, offering girls jobs at hotels or resorts. Other come in and take pictures of the girls and boys and offer them an opportunity to be a model or a movie star. The girls then show up in the city, expecting to start a career, and instead they are raped repeatedly and told that their families will be killed if they disobey their new boss."

She pointed to a picture of a girl who looked to be about ten years old. A chill run up my spine and the anxiety I had been feeling for months suddenly flared.

"This is Alexa. She was found chained in a hotel room by the authorities in Thailand. She was sold repeatedly as a virgin."

The girl had bruised olive-brown skin and large sunken eyes. I stepped back from the picture and rubbed my arms from a growing agitation.

"The traffickers make more money for the younger girls," Camille said, "and there is a myth in many countries that if you have sex with a virgin, you will be cured of AIDS."

My stomach was threatening to turn inside out. Of all the stories I had written, I had never come across one that felt so utterly inhumane.

"Does she now have AIDS?" I asked.

"Yes, many of them do; and they don't have the medication to treat the disease the way we do in the States."

"These children all look so young."

"They are. The schemes bring in kids that are barely in adolescence; the younger ones are most often sold by their parents or a relative." She pointed to the lines of pictures on the wall. "These children have all been adopted for less than $100, which is usually ten to twenty dollars more than the traffickers offer the family."

The college boy on the computer continued to click through news sites about the earthquake while Emma looked over his shoulder. Camille stayed focused on our conversation, connecting to me as she did in the store, as if I was the only one in the room.

"How often do you get calls?"

"We receive several a week. In the communities where we have connections, we are notified when a relative has been offered money for their daughter or son and are about to make the deal. We then send one of our representatives, like Jess, to pick up the child and escort him or her to a private home or boarding school, where they are educated through high school."

I looked over at the maps and saw the concentration of red dots in Asia, Mexico, and to my surprise, the United States. "How many children are in the program?" I asked.

"We currently have about nine thousand in schools worldwide. Not much, given that two million children are sold each year. But it's a start."

"It's more than a start," Emma said.

"But it is still only a beginning. We need to give children a safe place to grow up." Camille said, looking at Emma with soft eyes. "If not, they turn against themselves, and often others, and we lose the resources they bring to the world that we need right now."

Emma gazed at Camille with a pensive look. The energy between them held layers of warm undertones, making me realize how well these women knew each other.

"My son, Jess, left this morning to pick up a five-year-old girl just south of the San Diego border." Camille took a labored breath and sat down.

"The border is over nine hours away," Emma said. "I'm sure he's still on the road or pulled over somewhere."

Camille looked up at Emma, their eyes connecting like soft light beams. "The problem is, nobody knows what time he left."

"Does anybody know the extent of the damage yet?" I asked.

"The reports are still coming in," the boy said, looking at the computer screen as he clicked away on the keyboard. "We are monitoring the tweets in the area, the news, and the social media blogs. There are a few overpasses down on the I-5 freeway just before the border." He flipped around in his chair. "Tijuana took the greatest impact. Their infrastructure is so poor that most of the city is reporting damage." He looked back at his computer and clicked a button. "It's getting dark down there, so people are saying it's harder to see the extent of the damage."

"Keep me posted," Camille said. "And can you please keep trying to reach Jess's cell phone for me?"

"I'm not sure what good that will do, but I'll keep trying," the boy said.

We followed Camille out to the studio, where she resumed her seat at the easel. She picked up her brush and nervously dabbed at the mustard vase. "I'm sorry, Kate. If I had my wits about me, I'd give you a tour of the studio."

"Oh, no ... please don't worry about that."

A cell phone chimed from her jacket pocket. Emma's eyes widened. Camille looked at Emma and then at her phone.

"It's Maria. This is the fourth time she has called in an hour."

"Let me talk to her," Emma said.

"Hello?" Camille asked into the phone. "No, nothing yet."

Emma rolled her eyes. The squawking from the cell phone was loud enough to hear from across the room.

"I promise I will call as soon as I know anything." She hung up and took a deep breath.

"Tell Maria to call me if she needs to talk with somebody."

"She's just scared. She has plans for her and Jess to meet with a wedding photographer tomorrow night, and she's afraid he won't be home in time to make the appointment."

"That's what she's scared about?" Emma asked.

"We all handle these things in our own way," Camille said as she picked up her paintbrush and continued to dab at the canvas at a steady pace.

"Call me as soon as you hear anything," Emma said.

"You know I will."

The waitress delivered our pizzas as we walked out of the studio. Neither one of us were hungry at that point, so Emma offered the pizzas to a bearded man wearing tattered tennis shoes and three layers of multicolored shirts. Thank God Emma ordered sausage and pepperoni. He looked too hungry for basil and tomato.

The day had become a cold, foggy dusk. We made our way back up the trail. Emma's stride was shorter than before, her steps as soft as the tone of her voice. My pace was awkward and uneasy. With all that was going on with Camille and the earthquake, I was feeling like my presence was becoming an inconvenience.

"How long have you known Camille?" I asked as we walked up the hill.

"We have known each other for over forty years."

"Where did you meet?"

"Oh … our husbands flew together in the navy." She stopped walking for a moment, took a deep breath, and then started again. "He was killed in action shortly after Jess was born, and we became family after that."

I wasn't sure how to respond. My instinct told me to just stay quiet.

"I adopted my boys from Camille's program. We raised the kids together. Jess is very much a son to me, too." She let out a deep breath. "God, I hope he is okay. I don't think Camille would survive if something happened to him."

While she wondered about Camille, I wondered about Emma and if the situation with Jess was triggering her memories of losing Sarah.

"Where are your sons now?" I asked.

"Leo teaches at a boarding school outside Bangkok, where Camille takes the children in that region. My oldest son, Tai, works in San Francisco as a stockbroker." Emma pushed her hands deep into the pockets of her long canvas coat.

"We have been through a lot together," she said, going on about how her boys grew up with Jess and went to the same school. She spoke of the family trips they took and watching the boys go off to college. They supported each other through the death of Camille's parents, the loss of Emma's husband, and the stroke she suffered the following year. But there was no mention of Camille being there for her during the loss of Sarah. If they had known each other for over forty years, they would have been through that together, too. The picture in the hall of Emma and Sarah came to mind along with a craving to get back to her memoir.

"Camille has a heart like no one I have ever met. She is one of those people who can feel the pain of the world and turn it into compassion." Emma stopped for a moment and looked back down the trail. "I'm sorry. I've spent all this time rambling on about Camille, and I haven't had a chance to ask about you."

"Oh, that's all right. I am in awe of the organization she has put together."

"She has helped many children live a better life," she said.

"It's sad to think that people are willing to sell their children."

"Unfortunately, not everybody has parents who are capable of caring for them." Emma gave me a gentle smile as a nearby streetlight softly lit her face. "Are you close to your mother, Kate?"

"I never met my birth mother. She sold me the legal way—to a private adoption agency. I don't think I was quite the perfect child she wanted."

Emma gasped and stopped walking. "What makes you think that?"

"I didn't pass the ten toes and ten fingers count," I said, keeping my hands in my pocket.

"Oh … I can't imagine that would be a reason to not keep a child."

"I guess it doesn't really matter why. She died from what I think was a drug overdose a year after I was born, so I would have been adopted anyway. I'm just thankful for the parents I have. They're great people."

"Tell me about them."

"My mother is an investment banker, and I don't think she will ever retire. My dad is a history professor at a local college. He is probably also one of my best friends. I think that happens sometimes when you are an only child."

"What a wonderful thing to say about a parent," she said.

We walked the rest of the way without speaking, allowing our own sort of connection to form through the cold, quiet air. When we reached the house, Emma invited me in for tea.

"I'd love to," I said as the dogs came running out from the yard. With wagging tails that could trim the bushes, they followed us into the kitchen, sniffing the floor for treats. Emma filled an old iron teapot and flamed the stove with a wooden match.

"Once upon a time, this stove used to start itself. Now it's as old and stubborn as I am." She flipped open a notebook computer sitting on the kitchen table and scanned the latest updates on the earthquake before shutting the system down.

"I sure hope Jess gets out of there okay," she said, pulling tea leaves out of a drawer, speaking in a rapid stream of words that went from the earthquake to herbs to what kind of tea her husband used to drink. She had seemed calm during our walk home, but now her hands were shaking as she fumbled to put the teacup onto a tray. I wondered if she was more anxious about Jess, Camille, or entertaining me during such a tense time.

I turned off the stove, poured the hot water, and offered to carry the tray into the living room.

"Thank you. That would be helpful." Emma smiled and then looked past me. "Oh, yes, I'll need the papers," she said. She hurried into the alcove, picked up the stack of articles on her desk, and then slid the white envelope with my name on it into the top drawer.

We walked through the hall and into the spacious living room.

"I enjoyed looking at your pictures when I arrived. Your children are beautiful."

She nodded without expression. "Why don't we sit down here," Emma said, turning on a desk light and pointing to a couch and a pair of worn wingback chairs that faced the large stone fireplace. She lit the fire with a long match and sat down, crossing her legs toward me as she picked up her teacup from the tray and rested it on her thigh. I took the seat next to her and exhaled. The warmth of the fire on my legs continued to ease me, as did Emma's engaging smile. The moonlight coming through the skylight softened her strong features, and her face appeared younger, almost angelic.

"I'm sorry with all the commotion going on around us we haven't had a chance to talk about why I invited you here." Her eyes settled onto mine. Emma unfastened the paper clip around the articles. "I have a close friend who lives in New York. She sent me these a few months ago," she said, handing me the stack.

I scanned through the articles I had written for the *Journal*. I looked over the book review on Emma's latest publication on social change, an article on a teen group that participated in a causality study of its actions, and a phone interview I did with the sister of an Iranian woman who was murdered in a protest.

"I'm impressed by your point of view. You seem to be tapping into something I believe is very significant."

I nodded, wondering what it was about the articles she felt was so significant, not wanting to reveal that I wasn't putting the same dots together in my head. "I'm flattered that you like the articles and a bit curious why your friends chose to send them to you."

"She knows I'm looking for some good writers right now that have strong regional audiences like the *Journal*."

"It's not as strong as it used to be," I said. My fingers clenched around my teacup as I held in a breath. "Are you looking for journalists to write on a particular topic?"

"Yes, I am. And based on these articles, you would be perfect." She took another sip of her tea and then set it down to adjust the falling strands from her long, pulled-back hair. "There was another reason you came to my attention, but I believe that only reinforced that you are the one I need for the Eastern region."

"What was the other reason?"

"I'm not sure if that's important right now. Sometimes we are led to people or places not for the reason we think but for something more significant."

I looked down at my teacup, wanting to speak, wanting to tell her that I no longer worked at the *Journal*, but nothing came out.

"Does that interest you?"

"Interest me?"

"To write an article for the *Journal*. Does that interest you?"

"Of course." My stomach tensed as if I punched myself. "What do you want the writers to write about?"

"I think you are already tapping into it."

"I am?"

"Yes, but before I elaborate, we should probably get to know each other a little better. If we do, I believe something significant will emerge."

I sat back and took a sip of the tea, tightening my grip on the cup while trying to put pieces together that didn't fit. I had little if anything to offer a woman like Emma, and a few articles written for a regional publication didn't seem to make me an interesting enough person to warrant an invitation. "I'm not sure anything of much significance is going to emerge from me."

"I don't for a minute believe that. There are aspects in all of us that are trying to emerge. It's how we evolve."

I looked up at Emma and thought about a passage from her last book, about how people are forced by environmental factors or internal strife to mutate, to find a new form in which to function more efficiently, more at peace with their inner and outer environments. Her book made me realize that something inside of me was trying to evolve. Feelings of anxiety and conflict had been bubbling inside of me for months.

Warmed by the comforting tone of her voice, I felt myself open. "Sometimes I wonder if what is trying to emerge in me is not such a good thing."

Her eyes smiled, as if pulling me into a room within the room, thick with intimacy.

"You are not the first person to feel that way." She stood and walked toward the bookshelf. "There are women all through history who have resisted internal changes because they were afraid what was trying to emerge would be too disruptive or destructive to their lives." Emma pulled down a blue hardcover book from one of her shelves. "This is a wonderful read," she said as she handed the book to me. "It is about ten famous and not-so-famous people who experienced changes in their lives that ultimately aligned them with their contributions to society. They all thought in the beginning that the changes were not such a good thing."

The names were listed on the cover. I recognized Eleanor Roosevelt, Mother Theresa, Jonas Salk, and Elisabeth Kubler-Ross. "These are international figures; we know they made special contributions to the world," I said.

"Yes—however, the point of the book is not who they are but what they went through to become who they are. There are millions of people who are just as significant that you never hear about."

I opened the cover of the book.

"It's part of what I need my writers to write about," Emma said as she looked down at her watch. "But we can talk more about that in the morning. I thought we would get up early and take a hike in Big Sur."

"That sounds good to me. Do you mind if I take this book to my cottage?"

"Please. Feel free to read any of the books you find here."

I looked at her, wondering if on some level she was giving me permission to read her memoir. I felt eager to get back to the next chapter.

We took our cups to the kitchen and said good night. There was a strained distance between us, like resisting an urge. Something inside of me wanted to hug her good night. Something I saw in her eyes made me think she wanted me to.

A blustering sea breeze blew through the patio. The rustle of tall trees deepened the chill in my bones while I unlocked the door and returned to the cottage. I pulled off my sweater, wrapped the red quilt around my shoulders, and checked my cell phone. There was still no reception to reach David, and even if there were, I wasn't sure what I'd say. "There is something emerging in me that makes me not want to marry you" didn't seem like a good topic for a phone conversation.

I set down the book Emma gave me on the nightstand. How Jonas Salk and Elisabeth Kubler-Ross found their life purpose was not nearly as interesting to me as how Emma did. I quickly changed into my cotton pajamas and then sat up in bed, waiting for the lights to go out in the big house. When the patio went dim, I snuggled beneath the quilt and picked up her memoir, feeling a bit more at ease about reading whatever I found. I opened to the second chapter.

The gift of intolerance is the motivation it breeds. While Eastern Germany was filling with expressionless men toting long steel weapons and wearing heavy wool uniforms, my heart was filling with a deep anxiety that made it difficult to breathe. Yet it was not until my nineteenth year, the year the wall divided our flowerless city, that the intolerable acts forced upon me by my father and a growing sense of ambition to become a person of value turned into an undeniable courage to flee.

Hans, my childhood schoolmate, who loved me in ways I could not recognize, once again came to my aid. We shared, as only one can with a kindred spirit, a deep passion for aviation. The sights and sounds of planes screaming across the sky, freed from gravity, propelling themselves into wide open spaces, made one feel that life did exist beyond the perilous borders crafted of new ideologies. Hans and I studied the aviators of history, and long before the imprisonment of our city, we had drawn plans to create our own craft. For months, we collected dark rain gear. Susan, my younger sister of ten years, the child that became mine as my mother passed her last breath to me, was quiet and insatiably eager to please. Together we would work late into the night, cutting large squares out of the coats and sewing the linens tightly together, listening closely for the lumbering footsteps of our father returning from the local pubs, where he would meet with other men as fanatical as he about spreading the ideals of the governing power.

By late fall, Susan and I had sewn the clothes into a large open-mouthed balloon designed to capture enough hot air from a burning bed of coals to lift us over the twelve-foot wall and far into the green open fields of Western Germany. Our fingers wore the calluses of the thick yarn we pulled across our skin. Susan picked at hers until they bled, while I feared her nervous habits would somehow expose us to our father before I could get her to a place of safety I could only dream of in my mind.

The moon and the weather determined our launch, and in mid-November, the perfect night had arrived. With the help of Hans's brother, we carried the pieces of our craft to a small grove of trees just within the confines

of the wall. No one spoke as we stoked the hot coals that
fueled the balloon while securing the ties to a small plank
of wood that would carry us into the air.

A strong wind blew over the roof, shaking the window. I sat
up and adjusted my pillow, amazed that it was the first time I had
heard this story about Emma. I knew from a trip I had taken to
Berlin that several people escaped the eastern wall by crafting hot
air balloons. But somehow, she had kept her escape a secret. With
all her public service and diplomatic accomplishments, it was never
documented how she came from Eastern Germany. A lingering
chill ran up my arms. I pulled the covers closer to my neck and
continued to read.

> The moonless night was graciously frigid, and the cold
> air aided in a rapid ascent. Susan clutched her body
> around mine while Hans and I crouched on the small
> wooden plank holding the ropes that led to the balloon.
>
> The lift was so quiet, I could hear the heat rise. The
> floating sensation filled my body with exhilaration as we
> quickly rose over the shrinking wall and into the dark,
> clear sky. Susan continued to push herself so snug into
> my chest that for a moment, I lapsed to a place where we
> had no boundaries. She was the more timid side of me,
> the heart that remained open, the innocence I had lost
> so long ago that still shone through the dark rings of fear
> she too had beneath her eyes.
>
> A light breeze sailed us toward the western fields. The
> dimming lights of Berlin, east and west no longer visibly
> divided, was the last vision I had before our sovereignty
> was shattered by the piercing sound of gunfire. The deep
> trembling of shock and Susan squeezing her life into
> mine was the last thing I would remember for days.

A loud knock startled me out of the book. I stared at the door, and it rattled again.

"Kate, it's Emma."

I threw the manuscript under the covers, jumped up to toss my sweater over the broken chair, and then opened the door. Emma's face was barely lit by the dim porch light coming from the house.

"I just spoke to Camille. She still hasn't heard from Jess, and now there are reports of sweeping fires through the area. I don't want her to be alone tonight," she said, tying the long wool belt around her black coat, her hair blowing against her face from the wind. "I'll be back in the morning. If we hear from him, we will still be on for that hike."

"Do you want me to drive you? It's awfully dark and windy out."

"Oh, no. I'll be fine."

"Are you sure?"

"Positive." I looked down at Max and Sadie staring up at Emma.

"Do you mind if the dogs stay with me tonight?" I asked.

"No, not at all." She stepped into the cottage and called the dogs onto the round area rug on the floor. I froze staring at the frame of the manuscript popping up from under the flat quilt. "The house is open if you need anything." She said as she hurried to close the door behind her. I let out the breath I was holding while the dogs curled up as if they knew something frightening was happening. Max's long nose rested on the carpet, and his large brown eyes looked up at me.

"Everybody is going to be fine," I said, locking the door, feeling a subtle sense of dread that seemed to come with strong winds and shaky structures. The dogs and I looked at each other until the sound of her car faded. Then Max and Sadie closed their eyes. I thought about going into the house to turn on the news about the earthquake. It was what I should do, I thought. I should stay informed or at least more concerned—but with stories like that, I knew there wouldn't be concrete information until morning, and either way, they wouldn't be reporting on the whereabouts of Jess. I thought about Camille and the connection she had with Emma. I was thankful they had each other for the night. I jumped back into bed and pulled out the manuscript.

I awoke with both legs broken at the knees and ribs that stabbed at me like steel arrows with each shallow breath. Susan lay next to me in the back room of a small farmhouse, her frail young legs broken and bandaged, her shoulder disfigured as it concaved into her chest. She had been awake days before me. There was not a wince of pain, not a word, until we could speak. Our caregiver was Anna, a Swiss-German milk farmer whose gallant husband found us in their field early that fall morn. Hans was not with us. Nor did I hear again of his whereabouts. All that was left were the night terrors and the insatiable shame that perhaps my life was at the expense of his.

The door I had hoped to open by leaving my father behind was now coming to a close. I lived deep within my mind, keeping others at a safe distance while Susan clung to my side like a broken-legged lamb. Anna respected my silent boundaries while she nursed us back to health. Each day, she would carry us out to the red barn that smelt of souring cream and molting fowl. There she would insist that we walk around the tightly-bound hay, assisting ourselves as we maneuvered around the stacks. "We heal from the inside out," she would say as Susan winced to move in inches while I took large steps to complete the task, tightening my jaw to the bone, numbing the pain as I moved.

In the evening, she would read to us by the fire. The warmth of the burning embers crackled in my chest, where the deep ache for my mother would melt open and be known. I heard her soft, caring voice in Anna's. I could smell her skin in Susan's. The longing to return to her arms would deepen. I wanted only to be held again by her where my life after her death would mercifully disappear. At times such as these, my need for her became so intense that it threatened to break me open to bleed. Once again, I realized one cannot survive with such anguish in one's heart. I would need to find a way to wall off the loneliness I could no longer tolerate to feel.

My eyelids began to droop. I set the manuscript down by my side. The irony of Emma escaping one wall only to create another lingered in my mind with no place to put it.

Chapter 4

Susan and I arrived in New York two years after we left East Berlin, a year after meeting Jon. I knew I would marry him moments after settling my eyes in his, aware of the fierce soul beneath his blue uniform and alabaster skin. A slow sidewalk dance outside of our caretaker's café led to a deep yearning for his physical being and an emotional pull that inebriated me with a sense of reckless joy. I was too young to know of the true origin of this type of love, too naive to know that what lie latent in my psyche was about to uncoil like a hissing cobra provoked by any opening to love. We spent many nights in a small, dark room, lying naked under scratchy sheets and a heavy wool blanket that smelled of his mossy, sweet cologne. In his arms, I would slip into a world of silence, a stolen tranquility were no separation exists. This state that may well be heaven's doorway melted my identity in such a way that I didn't know or care who I was. Jon preferred me this way. I preferred it to be temporary.

By morning, I would surly flee to intimacy's polar opposite. Here I would busy myself in my work in the café and my studies with Susan. Her writing quickly became more than proficient for her age, which allowed me time to focus on my own.

I became increasingly passionate in my desires to free citizens from the authorities that enslaved them. At night I would bury myself in books, papers, and underground radio, keeping Jon and Susan close while at a comfortable distance. Susan and I found a passive connection in this proximity. Jon, on the other hand, wanted more.

THE MORNING LIGHT FILLED THE cottage, and I set down the manuscript and stared at the ceiling. Jon was starting to sound like David and Emma a bit more like me than I had imagined. The book fell to my side as a thought began to stir. Her experience continued to resonate inside of me. My mind struggling to connect to something that felt illusive.

Max's tail wagged across the floor as Sadie popped up onto the bed and shook herself awake. "You two want to go out?" I asked as I opened the door to the cold morning air. The dogs ran out in the yard, and I went to the edge of the porch and peeked around the corner toward the driveway. Emma's old box-style Mercedes was not in the turnabout. Wishing I had a hot cup of coffee, I headed back into the cottage and changed my clothes to go into the house.

The sound of car wheels rolling over gravel got louder as my head popped out of my sweatshirt. The car pinged and sputtered to a stop. A few moments later, the back door rattled open. I peered through the window. Max and Sadie stood on the patio, wagging their tails into each other until Emma, wearing the same coat she left in, dropped a cup of dog food into their steel bowls. She slid a smooth rock in the foot of the door to keep it from closing and then walked back into the kitchen. I tucked Emma's manuscript into the bottom of my luggage, pulled up my jeans, and headed out the door.

"Good morning," I said to Emma, watching her light the teapot.

"Oh, Kate, you're up early."

"Still on East Coast time. Did Camille hear from her son?"

"She received a text from Jess's phone. The message is garbled, so we can't read it, but at least he is communicating. Can I get you something to eat?"

"Oh, no. That's okay. Why would the text be garbled?"

"It's mayhem down there. There are so many people in the area trying to communicate at once that it's almost impossible to get clear information in or out."

"At least she is hearing something. That's good news."

"It is indeed. Now if I could just get Marie to calm down."

"Marie?"

"Jess's fiancée. She called a half a dozen times last night." Emma looked down at the dogs. Her long gray hair, pulled back in a tie with soft strands falling around her face, accented a look of perplexity I strained to understand.

"Camille's worried enough. She doesn't need that kind of provocation."

"Is Jess an only child?"

"Yes. And they are very close."

My chest swelled with a sense of Camille's strength. Given the number of children they had saved, she must have waited for Jess's return many times. I had long admired people who made such sacrifices even though it often made me feel like I was living life on the sidelines, avoiding the chance of a personal loss.

I looked over at Emma ripping tea leaves off a dry branch. Her forehead was strained like she was pondering a thought, and I wondered if the situation with Jess was making her think about Sarah.

"How does somebody deal with that?" I said without thinking.

She looked at me, her head slightly cocked. Then she looked away. "Anyway, I think we are fine to go on our hike. Are you still up for it?"

"Absolutely."

"Good. I think you will enjoy the area. You sure you don't want any coffee or breakfast?"

"Coffee sounds good. Can I make it?"

"Oh, no. I'll make you a cup." She crossed to the other counter and opened a white wood cabinet. "Oh, Kate, I meant to tell you that you are welcome to come in to watch the news or get on the Internet. Since you are out west, the *Journal* might need you to cover the earthquake."

My eyes darted down at the dogs. "Thank you, but they have other reporters for that." Max stared at me with his tongue hanging out. His big brown eyes were so pure with honesty that they begged me to find my own. "Do you mind if I use your phone, though? I can't seem to get cell coverage here."

"Of course." She pulled out a loaf of bread and directed me to the phone in the alcove off the kitchen.

I walked in the alcove and picked up the receiver on her desk, staring at the drawer where she slid the envelope the night before.

"Would you like mayonnaise and mustard on your sandwich?"

"Just mayonnaise." My fingers reached for the metal knob. I pulled it slowly and saw the edge of the white cover.

"How about tomatoes? I have a little basil if you'd like."

"No, that's okay." I closed the drawer and dialed David's cell. His recorder picked up. Where would he be on a Saturday morning? And why wouldn't he have his cell phone with him? A pang of longing tugged at my chest. If David was available, I was vaguely disinterested. If he wasn't, I ached to be with him. I hated both states of me and what it must be like for him to be pulled and pushed by extremes I pretended didn't exist.

"Hey, Dave, it's me. Just trying to reach you. I'll give you a call later. Miss you."

The receiver slid out of my hand and hit the floor before I could grab it. The crashing sound silenced Emma's humming.

"You okay?"

"Sorry. Just dropped the phone. I can be a little clumsy in the morning." I reached to the side of the desk for the receiver that had landed next to a stack of small framed photos. A black and white of Emma with Sarah smiling on her lap was on the top of the stack.

Above it was a set of small pinholes where the photos must have hung above her desk.

"So are you ready for a hike?" Emma asked as she stood in the doorway to the alcove.

I rose from the floor and hung up the receiver. "I think so. Will these shoes be okay?" I looked down at my white sneakers that were more suited for fashion than sports.

"Is that all you have?"

"It's the closest thing I have to hiking boots."

"Then they will work just fine."

We walked into the kitchen, and she handed me a blueberry scone off the counter that was wrapped in a gold cloth napkin. "You might want to get a little something in your stomach. We are heading down the coast highway, and the roads can get a little windy."

She set down a cup of coffee in front of me, steam rising from the rim with the smell of a dark roast. Emma packed sandwiches and an assortment of fruits in a bag; then she excused herself to change her clothes. I picked up my coffee, and the dogs followed me back to my cottage. The image of Sarah and Emma in the photo lingered with me as the morning sun burst through a dark cloud, inviting me to sit in the teak chair on the porch outside my room. I sat down and rested for a moment. I wanted to tell Emma about my job, but it felt too soon to risk losing her level of interest in me. I needed to keep building a bond with her so she would share more about her life—not just about Sarah, but about how she became who she was.

A phone began to ring. The sound was coming from a half-opened window in the cottage next to mine. There were a few more loud rings, and then a recorder picked up. There was a beep, and then the voice of somebody leaving a message: "Hello, Mrs. Davis, this is Steven Demarco from the *Journal*."

I stood up from the chair and walked toward the window. "I think there has been a bit of a mix-up. Kate Edwards no longer works at the *Journal*, and we will be sending ..."

Bang! The warped back door to the house crashed open, and Emma stepped onto the patio. I leaped off the porch, my coffee spilling as I fast-walked toward her. "Are we ready to go? To Big Sur? On the hike? Should we take the dogs or some extra water? What did you need me to do to help? Here, why don't you let me carry the backpack."

She gave me a perplexed look while I stretched my neck and listened to make sure the message was over.

"I thought you New Yorkers could handle your coffee."

"Good point. We usually can. But there is something about jet lag and coffee and going on a hike with a lot of trees that can make us a little nervous. By the way, is this one of those hikes where you are hanging off a steep cliff? Or one with a wide path and little slopes?"

Emma gave me a comforting smile. "The paths change all the time up here. We learn to adapt." Emma lifted the pack onto her shoulder and started walking toward the car. I lingered for a moment, gazing through the half-opened window of the cottage.

"Come on, Kate. A storm is supposed to come in later today. We need to get moving."

Sadie and Max were waiting at the car, their tails wagging as they watched Emma load the trunk. "Sorry, doggies. You don't get to go this time." She slammed the back trunk several times before the rusty hinge closed. "Now you two be good. We'll be back in a few hours."

The car sputtered to a start, and we headed south. To the east were hills covered with redwood trees separated by lush green golf courses that ran to the edge of the ocean. Emma encouraged me to finish my scone as we entered the Big Sur region, where the roads narrowed to single lanes carved from jagged cliffs that snaked high above the coastline. I balanced the sway of my coffee as the Mercedes tilted from side to side while my head ached, thinking what to do about the phone message from Steven.

"How did you sleep, Kate?"

"Excuse me?"

"Did you sleep well?" she said.

"Oh…pretty good. It's very quiet here."

"My favorite part of living here is the quiet and that every day of the year, there is the most delightful scent of pine and sea breeze in the air."

"Have you lived here long?"

"Long enough to call it home."

I looked out the window, feeling the numbness of my skin as I dug a fingernail into the palm of my hand. *I've got to get rid of that message.* "Were the cottages on the property here when you bought the house?"

"No. Jon and I built those a few years after we moved in. Jon was much more of an extravert than I am. He loved to have people over. These days I use the middle one for an office and keep the guest list to a minimum." The car swerved to the right. Emma jerked to adjust the wheel after crossing over the yellow line. "Sorry about that. You don't always see the curves coming."

"No, you don't," I said as my stomach tightened another notch. "You don't happen to have a scanner in that office? I'd like to send something back to New York today."

"I have one in the house. The cottage office is a mess right now. I'd be embarrassed for you to go in there."

I took a shallow breath. "That's okay. It can probably wait until Monday."

"Most things usually can," she said, the side of her mouth etching up like a sliver moon. "Do you hike at all in New York?"

"I jog occasionally through the park but can't say I've done much hiking."

"The trails around here used to be spectacular this time of year, but unfortunately, the fires have damaged or destroyed many of the trees." Emma pointed out to a distant ridge that looked like a tattered row of black sticks stretching toward the sky for mercy.

Passing over a suspended bridge, she turned off the road and sped past a *Closed* sign that hung on the guard shack to the park entrance.

"There is a trail just behind those trees. It may be a bit muddy, but it will get us to the top of the ridge."

Emma grabbed her pack out of the backseat and then excused herself to call Camille. I looked up at the sky. Clouds to the north were darkening like billows of black steam broken by tracks of blue before merging with another heap of darkness. The storm seemed to quickly double its mass as it grew as large as the northern skies. Oddly, the tall redwoods next to me barely moved, as if a pressure system was holding off the inevitable eruption. I bent down and tightened my shoes, pulling the laces so hard my socks bunched at the sides.

Emma returned a few minutes later from the edge of the parking lot. "Still nothing more from Jess," she said. "I told Camille we would stop by when we finish the hike." She looked down at my feet. "Hope you didn't pay too much for those shoes." Emma opened the trunk to pull out her walking stick and began a stride that I struggled to maintain.

We headed up the mountain along a rushing creek on a narrow trail that was barely distinguishable among the overgrown ferns and flowers that canvassed the canyon floor. The darkening clouds now loomed over the canopy of redwood trees, most of which were scorched halfway up their towering trunks. Other trees were torched to the crown and had fallen like black pick-up sticks scattered through the forest.

"This is so tragic," I said, "and oddly beautiful at the same time."

"That it is."

We meandered up switchback trails that were partially destroyed. At points, the path was impassable, which seemed to be a minor inconvenience for Emma as she climbed around boulders, mudslides, and fallen trees, forging new trails as she navigated up the hill.

"I read in an article that you are originally from Germany."

"I see you have done your homework."

"Is that where you met your husband?"

"I did. He was stationed there for a few years prior to going to Vietnam."

There was much written about Emma and her trip to rescue her husband after the war. It felt like a safe topics that might create a deeper conversation. "Do you mind if I ask you about Vietnam?"

"You might as well. Everybody does."

"After the navy declared him dead, how did you know he was still alive?"

She let out a breath that sounded like a soothing hum. "I felt it. Then I dreamt about him. Then I received a call from a friend of his who told me where he was."

"And how did you get the plane?"

"I flew into Thailand and rented one." She told the story of her night flight into the jungle as if she had told it so many times that it bored her. As she spoke, I felt like I was a journalist with her, and I didn't like the feeling. She stopped walking and looked back at me. "Would you like to know what he looked like when I found him? Or can we skip that part."

"We can skip that part," I said.

Her lips pushed opened into a smile of gratitude.

"You were very courageous." I added.

"Not really. Losing Jon felt more painful than dying trying to find him. Back then, they called that love. Today, I think they call it codependence." Her breath let out a chuckle. She planted her pole and turned toward the trail. "Have you always lived on the East Coast?" she asked.

"I grew up in a small town in Virginia and then moved to Syracuse to start college."

"Virginia is a beautiful state. What town are you from?"

"Oakbridge."

"That's just outside of the capitol, isn't it?"

"About thirty miles. Have you been?"

"No," she said, shaking her head. "Never have. But I knew somebody who lived there. Have you ever heard the name Susan Webber?"

"Susan Webber? Sounds like a teacher in my elementary school, but I can't say I could put a face to her. Why?"

"Just wondering." The lilt in Emma's voice began to fade. The incline increased, and I began to wonder if I was who she thought I was—or who she wanted me to be.

"How is your job at the *Journal* going?"

"Ahhh ..." I yelled as I slipped down the slope several feet before catching myself on a tree. Emma stepped down the hill and reached out her hand. "That's okay. My shoes are just a little slippery." We side-stepped back up to the path, and Emma slowed her pace.

"The *Journal* has a great deal of appeal to me. Like I said last night, it has a strong circulation in the Northeast region for the audience I'm trying to reach."

"What's the topic you want your writers to write about?"

Emma stopped and looked back at me. "We will get to that."

I nodded, choking off the frustration with my breath. She was testing my patience, or lack of it, and it felt as deliberate as her stride.

"What else do you like to do when you're not working?" Emma asked.

"I guess I like to read. And sometimes I like to golf with my dad."

"Your dad's a golfer?"

"He used to play more. But he's been pretty ill lately."

"Oh ... I'm sorry to hear that."

I kept my eyes fixed to the trail while Emma dipped under a low branch and then held it high until I passed through. "There's another wash-out ahead. It's probably best to just follow the tree line," she said as she opened her backpack and handed me a thermos of water.

"Any chance we could get lost up here?" I asked.

Emma looked around the forest and then back at me. "We're probably already lost. But don't worry; I'll get you home." She pushed off her stick and headed up the hill. I looked down the mountain in search of the parking lot. The only sight behind us was a blanket of treetops. My breath began to shorten, and I hurried my pace to walk by her side.

We headed up a partial trail with a smaller incline along a glassy stream that rushed through rocks and brought the crisp smell of moisture to the air.

"So it must have been interesting being a US ambassador at such a young age."

"I think it would be interesting at any age," she said, then put her hand up like a traffic guard and went still. I stood behind her, waiting to see what she saw. There was a crackle in the trees on the slope above the trail. A moment later, a buck twice the size of Emma bolted out in front of her and leaped down the hill, the muscles in his hind legs sculpted like tight ropes in spotted brown fur.

"Look at him go." She shook her head and kept walking. "Jon and I used to take this hike on Sunday mornings. Back then, the deer would walk right up to you and eat an apple out of our hand. Now they are all so spooked."

"From the fires?"

"Most likely. Animals sense so much."

"Your husband sounds like he was a wonderful man. How long has it been since he passed away?"

Emma squinted as she cocked her head, as if she knew I was asking questions I already had the answers to. "He passed away over a decade ago. How about you? Are you married?"

"Engaged."

"Ah, the brilliant bless of new beginnings. When is the wedding?"

"Well, we haven't exactly set a date yet."

"What's the fellow's name?

"David."

Emma looked at me and nodded. "Well, no reason to rush into life choices," she said. She planted her stick in the ground and started up the final incline. "What does David do for a living?"

"He's an attorney."

"Not a bad occupation."

Sadness tugged on my heart with the thought of David. I took another step to move past it when a butterfly blew down the path and banked off my arm. Three more flew over my head as we reached the top of the forest and the brush became dry and less dense. Butterflies were sprinkled through the air, followed by what seemed like an endless stream of the fluttering insects.

"Have you ever seen the migration of the monarch butterfly?" Emma asked.

"No, I can't say I have."

"Well, you are in for a treat. This is my favorite time of year up here," Emma said as we popped out of the brush and were greeted by the grandeur of a wavy blue ocean that stretched wide and deep into the line of the darkening horizon. Flocks of butterflies now filled the air, all fluttering like drunken sailors as they made their way north toward thick, dark clouds gliding down the coast.

Emma took a seat on a large, flat rock that looked over the sea. I sat across from her, not wanting to get too close to the edge. She opened her pack and offered me a turkey sandwich that looked like the ones my mom used to put in my lunch pail—a layer of thinly-pressed white meat on wheat bread with a bead of mayonnaise oozing out the sides. I took a bite and looked out to the horizon. Beyond the stream of butterflies, two white spouts rose from the face of the ocean.

"What are those spouts?" I asked.

"Ahh … that is why I love this time of year. They are from the blue whales that are migrating south to Baja to give birth to their young. Thousands of whales make the journey every year, and for the next few weeks, we are blessed to watch the butterflies fly north while the whales swim south," she said as she unwrapped her sandwich.

I looked out to sea. The smallest and largest of creatures moved according to their instincts while I was denying my own.

"So tell me more about David," Emma said.

I looked at her as she looked through me. I was used to asking the questions, and it felt oddly vulnerable to be on the receiving end of the process. "He is a good guy," I said. "I'm just not sure if I am ready to be married yet. Maybe I am just a restless soul."

"What makes your soul restless," she asked, "besides being a journalist in New York?"

"I don't know. I guess I have always been this way, but lately, it's worse."

"What's worse?"

"A feeling of anxiety. For the past several months, I have felt very unsettled."

"That makes sense."

"It does?"

"There is often a rise in anxiety before a person or a society goes through a significant evolution."

"Like getting married?"

"Certainly that could be a cause, but it's usually associated with a larger sense of one's self, not necessarily associated with another. Did you have a chance to read the book I showed you last night?"

"No, not yet."

"You might find something helpful in there." She pulled out an orange and peeled it with a small pocket knife in one long, curving strip. I took a bite of my sandwich and washed it down with some tea.

"I do love the timing of things." She closed up her thermos. "Have you ever seen the way silver is cleaned?"

"No, I can't say that I have."

"It's melted down in a vat. The silver maker then turns up the heat so the impurities that are imbedded in the metal float to the top. Everything that is not authentic can then be seen and removed."

Losing my job sure turned up the heat. And then there was David. I looked over at Emma. "What if when the heat turns up, you have to remove a person?"

She chuckled, tipping her head toward the sky. "Ah ... if only it were that easy. People only reflect what is inside of us. You can remove somebody, but what that person represents to you or what they show you about yourself will still remain." A raindrop fell on my arm, and then another on my nose. I stared out at the ocean.

"How do you remove the impurities?"

"There are lots of ways," she said as she packed her bag. "If you're up for it on Sunday, we can head over to Big Basin. I'll show you a process one of my friends uses."

"Is she a silver maker?"

Emma smiled. "When it comes to people, she is."

She sounded like somebody I needed to meet. But if Emma picked up that phone message from Steven, I might not be around by Sunday.

"The story you would like published—does it have to do with the events in your life?"

Emma's high cheeks pulled toward the ground. She glared out to the ocean and then bent down to tighten the laces on her hiking boots. Dark rain clouds now covered the sky, and a spattering of large drops began hitting the ground.

"Kate, there are far more important things happening in the world right now than the events in my life." She took a deep breath and then stood and picked up her walking stick. "Come on. We should probably get out of here."

A loud crack of lightning speared out of a dark cloud, and large drops of water began to splash down. The last bite of my sandwich felt as if it was lodged in my throat. I swallowed hard and decided it was probably best to stay quiet for a while.

The rain began to pour. We scurried to pack our bags. Our hair was now flattened and dripping across our faces as we ran back into the forest for cover. Emma shouted through the rain, "Let's head down the north side! The trees will give us some cover!" We hurried down the first slope that was now a mud-drenched slip-and-slide.

"Oh, oh … damn …" *Splash.*

"Are you okay?" Emma yelled through the downpour while I sat up on the muddy trail.

"Yeah. I'm fine."

She waved me up to where she was standing. "Stay closer behind me."

"I'm okay."

"I know you are. I just want you to break my fall."

I adjusted my pack and wiped a layer of mud off my backside. We slowed the pace, and Emma braced us down the mountain, firmly planting her walking stick as she made large strides in the mud. The rain never let up; nor did the explosions of lightning followed by almost instant roars of thunder that lit up the dim forest. My heart was beating so fast I wondered at one point if Emma could hear it; then I looked at her during a flash of lightning and saw her laughing like a child. "There is nothing better than a good cleansing from Mother Nature!" she yelled.

"Yeah … nothing better." *If we survive it.* My senses heightened to detect every sound and smell in the forest as we headed down the hill to the orchestra of the storm. At the bottom, we turned a narrow corner and went down a steep decline toward the forest floor. My right foot slipped several times at the top of the slope. I shifted my weight to get more traction and then stepped on something slippery. Before I could gain my balance, both feet slid out from underneath me. My backside hit the trail, and sliding like a luge down an icy slope, I felt myself crashing at full speed into the back of Emma's knees.

"Whoa … whoa … whoa!" she yelled as her toes flipped up toward the sky and her body flew horizontally toward the trail before landing on mine. I was now a human sled with one arm around Emma's waist and the other reaching out to grab anything attached to the earth as we careened down the narrow slope and toward the rushing creek at the forest floor. My good hand scraped across rocks and twigs before landing on a thick exposed tree root that ran parallel to our descent. I grabbed the root at the top, and we jerked to a stop just before the creek. The forest went still.

"Uh-oh," Emma said with a lilt.

"Are you okay?"

"I don't like the sound of that."

"What?"

"Listen."

The rain had stopped, and the quiet was piercing. Small drops of water were now white noise to the crackling sound of a large redwood tree. An inner voice I did not recognize as my own gave me a firm and steady command. *Stay still. Don't move.* Emma didn't flinch, as if she was hearing the same voice. There was another large crack, and then a sound like a slow swinging door rang through the air while a huge redwood tree just left of our path began its fall into the dense burnt forest.

My panic subsided to sheer astonishment as the forest seemed to open in reverence to its falling elder. Gravity was now escalating the speed of the tree. Emma and I lay motionless, breathless. My eyes fixed on the massive trunk as it crossed over our path, crashing into the steep slope just above our heads, the ground vibrating from its impact.

Emma turned to me with a grin. "Do you think that's why the trail was closed?"

I nodded, wondering if Emma came into my life to enlighten me—or kill me. She turned to get up and winced.

"Are you okay?"

She reached for her knee and released a deep, audible breath.

"Oh, no! Did I slide into your bad knee?"

Her eyes squinted, giving me a perplexed, anguished look.

"I mean, are you okay?"

She looked up at the sky. Her jawbone protruded as she clenched her teeth. "We might have a little problem on our hands."

"What's that?"

"I can't seem to move my leg."

Chapter 5

DRIZZLE CAME DOWN IN PRISMS of light, illuminating the moisture in the air. Emma directed me to the river, where I ran to collect mounds of cold mud to pack in a paste around her swelling knee. I chewed on my lip as I scooped the wet dirt into my arms and up against my belly. *I can't believe I ran into her knee. God, can this get any worse?* I returned to find her sitting on the path, grimacing as she tried to move.

"Here, let me help you with that," I said, dropping the mud into a pile.

"It's not your fault, Kate. These trails are slippery."

There was something about her words that I didn't believe. Or maybe it was that she wouldn't look me in the eyes. We packed the mud on together, her breath deepening while she lifted her leg at the thigh, moving it up and down to loosen the joint. I held the base of her calf with both hands, guiding the leg where she directed it to go. It wasn't long before she had a range of motion that made her feel she could walk out of the forest. I tucked my shoulder into the pit of her arm; her right hand trembled to keep her weight on the walking stick while I lifted her up, keeping her snug by my side. There was something about holding her so close to me, using my strength to give her assistance, that made me feel more at ease—more real, more myself.

"You're stronger than you look," she said.

"Yeah, I've been told that before. How's the knee?"

"It will be fine. We just need to keep walking."

We hobbled along the river and out of the forest, Emma carrying most of her own weight by the time we reached the parking lot. There was a hose by the empty rancher station we used to wash off the mud. I ran to get a towel and a couple of sweatshirts Emma had in the back of her car while she leaned against a green metal picnic table and called Camille. I was so focused on the task that I was back before I could get cold.

"Did you reach her?" I asked, handing her a yellow towel as she put her phone back in her bag.

"Yes. She hasn't heard anything more." Thick lines on her brow furrowed into a track. She stared off toward the ocean with what was becoming a familiar pensive gaze. The trancelike state gave me a brief glimpse into her complexities, a world I could so far only access through her memoir. Her stare broke, and she limped toward the car. "Do you mind if we stop by Camille's on the way home?" she asked.

"No, not at all. Are you okay?"

"I'm fine. Just a little swelling."

"Do you need me to drive?"

Emma looked down at her knee and then at me. "That might be a good idea." She handed me the keys and limped over to the passenger side. I walked around and opened the door for her. She still wasn't making eye contact, and I couldn't tell if it was because of her pain or because she thought I was becoming one. I offered her my arm, and she used it to brace herself as she moved down into the seat.

We listened to the news as we headed up the coast. The death toll was rising from the earthquake, and a large chemical explosion in Tijuana was adding to the numbers.

Emma dialed through several different radio stations, hoping to hear of a help or support line for families to make connections. All we heard were similar reports of the damage and devastation. Had I been there, I would have been reporting the same news, trying to provide the breaking story with more stats and more updates with the same level of intensity and insensitivity to the listeners who feared their loved ones might have just perished. I lost the appetite I had gained from the hike and started to feel tired and sleepy as the old car pinged and panged into the outskirts of town.

"Turn left at that next light," Emma said. "Camille's house is at the end of the street."

I pulled up to her small gray cottage with white trim. Rose bushes were budding along a mossy brick path that led to the front door.

"I'm just going to run in and check on her. Do you mind staying in the car?"

"You sure you don't need help?"

"No. My knee is already feeling better," she said, choking off a wince that turned into a grunt under her breath. She used her walking stick to help herself out of the car.

I nodded and swallowed hard, suddenly wishing my dad was sitting next to me. As overprotective as he was, to the point of me feeling crippled when I was determined not to be, he also was good about reminding me about things that were important, like not to take what other people did or said personally. That was a hard one for me—especially when it came to Emma.

I watched her hobble up the path and disappear behind the door. I rested my head against the window and thought about the message from Steven. *I have to just tell her I don't have my job anymore, apologize, and go home. Or maybe I should call Steven and beg for my job back so I can write whatever story Emma wants me to write for the* Journal. At that point, I just wanted to help her with whatever message she felt passionate about. And it was unlikely that message had anything to do with Sarah.

Emma's cell phone began to vibrate on the dashboard. It rang several times and then stopped. Moments later, it rang again as the caller called back. *What if it's news about Jess?* I looked at the front door, still half open. My mind wrestled with the risks of ignoring the call versus going up to the house uninvited. Ignoring the call seemed worse, so I picked up the phone and walked to the entry. The white wood door was ajar. I knocked a few times and then pushed the door open to a small, dim living room. The drapes were pulled shut. A set of three round candles were lit above the fireplace, encircled by rosary beads. In the corner was a TV on a small stand tuned onto a news station. A reporter was interviewing people on the streets in Tijuana while I heard voices rising in the back bedroom. I stepped closer to the hall.

"It's too soon."

"No, it's not. All she wants is the story. I can taste it. She's just like the rest of them."

"That doesn't matter."

"It does to me. She needs to want more than that."

"Give it more time."

A door opened. I stepped back, and Camille walked into the living room.

"Oh, Kate! I didn't know you were here."

"Somebody is trying to get a hold of Emma. I thought it might be important."

Emma limped out of the back room, her eyes avoiding mine as she reached for the phone and listened to the message.

"Can I get you something to drink?" Camille asked while a car with a loud engine roared into the driveway. The screech of sliding wheels pierced the air, then the slamming of a door. Camille looked at me with a furrowed brow. The loud clicking of heels clamored up the walkway, and the door was pushed open.

"Where is he?" the woman asked as she stormed into the room, her dark, wavy hair flowing down her pear-shaped body.

"I promised you that as soon as I hear anything I will call you," Camille replied.

"You were the one that sent him there. You need to be the one that finds him."

66

Emma set down the phone and stared into the eyes of the woman.

She ignored Emma as she raked her eyes down my body then up again to my face.

"Marie, this is Kate," said Camille.

I reached out my hand to greet her. She stared at my fingers and then crossed her arms across her body.

"What are you doing here?" she asked.

A long pause filled the air. I stepped toward her and smiled. "I'm a journalist with *Bride Magazine* from New York," I said. "I'm interviewing the mothers of only sons to see what kind of relationship they expect to have with their new daughters-in-law."

Camille took a sip of her water while Emma's eyebrows rose with a look of delight.

"Camille and I have a great relationship," she said, softening her tone.

"Interesting, because that's what we are finding. So far the brides and mothers-in-law we are interviewing have all said they share a genuine kindness and caring that reflects the special connection they have with their sons."

"Camille and I have that same relationship. I mean, it's tense right now with Jess missing, but we do have a great relationship."

Emma turned away and limped into the kitchen.

"This is a really difficult time. When are you going back to New York?"

"I'll be here for a few more days."

Marie looked at her watch. "I have a hair appointment in a few minutes. We are meeting with our wedding photographer tomorrow. I sure hope Jess gets home by then."

"You'll have to send me a picture," I said.

"That's a great idea. Can you put it in the article?"

"I'll see what I can do."

She grabbed her leather bag and walked out the door, yelling goodbye to Camille in a high-pitched voice that sounded as contrived as her concern.

Emma limped out of the kitchen, shaking her head. "I don't see what Jess sees in that woman."

"You need to get off that knee and get some ice on it," Camille said.

"I don't need ice."

"Yes, you do, and quit being so damn stubborn."

Emma lowered herself onto a dining room chair, tilted her head as she looked at me, and smiled. "*Bride Magazine?* That was brilliant." She lifted her water glass in a salute.

My shoulders let down as I exhaled, feeling relieved that we had reconnected.

"That was Jack Lo on the phone," she said to Camille, who was returning with a bag of ice to set around Emma's knee. "He didn't get the check for the girl's family in Thailand. His flight leaves on Sunday night, and apparently, the sex traders are becoming more aggressive. If he doesn't make it there by Tuesday, he thinks we might lose her."

"I mailed the check last week."

"It's probably just hung up at post office." Emma looked over at me. "If Kate doesn't mind driving me up to San Francisco, I can bring him the cash this evening."

"I don't mind at all."

Camille raised her eyes to the three candles burning over her fireplace. Pictures of her brown-skinned, dark-haired son in sturdy silver frames reflected the flickering flames. "I have to stay here."

"I know you do." Emma said. "Kate and I will make sure Jack gets the money." She stood and pulled Camille into her arms.

I looked down at the floor until the silence in the room filled with breaking news.

"A new report has just released on the latest death toll from the border quake ..."

Camille pulled away from Emma and toward the TV.

"Officials are now estimating that over three thousand lives have been lost, and the number missing is still unknown, as fires have hampered rescue missions in most of Tijuana."

Emma limped toward Camille and reached for her hand. "He is going to be okay," Emma said. "Jess knows how to get himself out of situations like these. I'm sure he will be home soon."

Emma rested the ice bag on her knee as we drove back to the house, sharing that she was far more concerned about Jess than she was letting on in front of Camille.

"It's unlike him to not make every effort to call his mom," she said. "He knows how much she worries about him."

"It sounds like he's been trying."

"Yes. I just wish the calls would come through," she said as we reached the roundabout.

I pulled the car to a stop, and Emma asked me to keep the engine running. She directed me to a shower in the house and said that she needed to go to the bank to get a money order for Jack. My offer to drive her was graciously turned down. I sensed that she either needed to be alone or was heading back to spend more time with Camille.

"We will need to leave here in about two hours," she said, wincing her way into the driver's seat.

"I'll be ready. Are you sure you don't want me to drive you?"

"No. I've driven in worse condition."

She put the car in gear and drove off. A wind of dust clouded the air while I stood in the roundabout, watching my life move in a circle that was beginning to strangle me. We were going to San Francisco on business, which meant there could be documents, and if she didn't get a copy of the money order at the bank, she would need to go into her cottage office and make one. *The last thing anybody needs right now is for her to pick up that message from Steven.*

I walked around the house, into the yard, and took off what was left of my shoes. Sadie and Max sniffed at my legs while I stared at the office cottage. *I need to get in there.* My small fingers curled up and scratched against my palm. She didn't want me to go into the office because it was messy. She didn't actually say to not go in. Thoughts of justification failed to ease my guilt; yet I knew I was going to do it anyway, so I might as well get it over with.

I walked up to the door of the cottage office and twisted the knob. It was locked. I knocked my forehead against the door a few times before bending toward the mat. I looked under it for a key and found nothing but a pair of silver bugs racing to find cover. Somehow, I knew this was not going to be easy. I walked around to the half-open side window and stared up through the pane. If I stood on something, I could pull down the glass and shimmy myself through the opening. I thought of using the chair I had already broken as a ladder before skimming the yard for a better choice. My eyes locked onto the steel trash can next to the kitchen door where Emma kept the dog food.

"Hope you two don't mind if I use your food for a minute."

The dogs followed me to the back door, their tails clanging against the bucket, while I dragged the heavy can across the patio and underneath the window. I unlocked the bottom portion of the window, pulled it up, and then slithered my damp body into the dark, musty room.

There were two wooden desks up against adjacent walls. In the corner was a tier of office equipment. On the top was a phone recorder with a cordless receiver. A red light flashing on the machine heightened my focus. I studied the recorder and then hit the play button. Every word Steven spoke dragged on like a stomach flu.

"Push two to erase, three to save." I tapped two with the tip of my index finger, picked up the receiver, and called him. After four rings, he picked up.

"Hello, Steven. This is Kate Edwards."

"Kate, what a surprise. I didn't expect a call from a *New York Times* reporter today."

I dropped my head as my hair fell around my face. "I need a favor."

"I'm sure you do."

"I am staying with Emma Daines this weekend, and she wants me to write a story for the *Journal*. If I can have my job back, I'll bring you the story and write articles on any assignment you give me."

Laughter blared through the phone—laughter that turned into more laughter. "I'll tell you what," he said. "You bring me back the story about what happened to her daughter, and you can have your job back. In fact, you bring me that story, and I will even give you your old pay."

"And if I can't?"

"Lose my number."

I took a deep breath. "Okay. Give me until Monday."

He hung up the phone, and I set the receiver back on the cradle. My mind went blank. I didn't know what to do, but I had two more days to figure it out. At least that would give me more time to repair the mess I had created with Emma.

A white cotton robe was hanging by the small sink in my cottage. I grabbed it along with a towel and went into the bathroom next to the kitchen. The dogs curled up on the floor outside the door while I stepped into the hot shower and melted a layer of dirt away. The hard water pelting down on my head rushed down my shoulders, stinging the open scrapes across my arms. I glided a bar of soap over my chest, hoping to remove the slime I felt from hearing Steven's voice. I never wanted to work for him again. But if I could get my job back, I could write the article Emma wanted published in the region. I washed and then rinsed out my hair, combing through the stubborn tangles with my fingers, pulling out a twig that fell to the drain. I turned off the water and grabbed a towel off the shower door. Ironically, I could only help her now if I could write the story about Sarah. *Maybe I should just tell her the situation.* Or maybe what I needed was in her memoir. I stepped out of the shower, put on the robe, and wrapped my wet hair up in a towel.

There was knocking at the back door. Sadie cocked her head at me as I walked into the kitchen. Max stood, wagging his tail. I tightened the robe around my waist and looked out the window. On the other side was a man with a cowlick in his dark, wavy hair and a wiry beard that grew into his chest. He peered through the window, waving his hand as if he was trying to show me he was friendly. I looked down at the dogs, both wagging their tails at the door.

"Can I help you?" I said through the glass.

He lifted a stack of papers. "I need to leave this for Emma."

"Okay. Just leave it at the door."

He looked down and then back through the window. "It's kind of wet out here," he yelled through the glass pane. "Do you mind if I come in?"

I looked at the dogs, they would have barked if he wasn't familiar so I opened the door. He wiped off his hiking boots and stepped into the kitchen, pearls of rain running down his heavy green jacket.

"Hi," he said, shifting the stack of papers under one arm as he reached out the other to shake my hand. "I'm Matt, a friend of Emma's."

I smiled, wrapped my arms around the waist of my robe, and took a step back. He walked into the kitchen and toward the counter.

"I'll just leave this here. Tell Emma we are ready to shoot the interview whenever she is finished with the final edits. But tell her there is no hurry. I know she is probably worried about Jess."

I looked down at the stack of papers, and my mind began to race. His thick brown hair and lean body made him look to be more of Jess's age than a contemporary of Emma's. "Are you a friend of Jess's?"

"Best friends. I was going to go with him to Mexico, but I had to finish this script. It's just killing me now that I'm not with him." He pulled out his keys and started slapping the leather tassel against his palm. "God, I hope he's okay."

I nodded, feeling awkward that I didn't know Jess—or anybody else in Aptos, for that matter. "Are you making a film?"

"It's a documentary," he said as he stepped back toward the door.

"Are you the writer?" I asked.

"Writer, producer, photography, trash-taker-outer, pencil sharpener, and sometimes I'm Emma's dog walker," he said as he reached down and petted Max behind his ears. "How about you?"

"Oh, I'm sorry. I'm Kate. I am staying with Emma for the weekend."

"The reporter from New York?"

"You know about that too?"

"Small town," he said as he reached over and picked up Sadie. "Well, I'm sorry to interrupt you. Thanks for letting me in." He opened the door, and Max followed him out. I walked out onto the patio with a list of questions on my tongue as he headed under the lattice archway to the driveway.

"Hey, what's your documentary about?" I yelled.

"The Esalen Indians," he said as he turned toward me and started walking backward toward the roundabout. "They used to live in this region." He tripped over a rock that bordered the path and flipped around to regain his balance without ever losing his cadence. "Bye, Kate," he yelled, waving his arm in the air as he jogged away.

I stood for a moment, wishing we had more time to talk. There was an ease about him that seemed to match the landscape, and it struck me as interesting that he was writing about the local Indians. I returned to my cabin and jumped into bed. The cold air pierced my damp skin and made me shiver. I pulled the quilt around my legs, reached down to my open luggage, and pulled out the memoir. I resisted the urge to skip ahead to find anything about Sarah. How Emma dealt with Jon's desire to have more of her had me curious all day.

> Jon and I married in the spring, and the wedding seemed to create another tear in the fiber that connected Susan and I. She didn't care for Jon's boisterous charm or his overzealous family, who took over our lives the day we engaged. By summer, his father had begun lobbying for Jon's post-military political career, I was awarded a scholarship to Harvard University, and Susan was placed in a nearby boarding school.

My precious sister, who was once quick to laughter, showed no emotion as I moved her into the small room at the all-girls campus in Connecticut. She too had found the escape of reading and never as much as pulled her freckled nose from the pages as I rubbed her head good-bye. I left the small dorm room as if my feet were sticking to the wood. One struggles at times such as these to know what is more painful—to be left or to leave. Beneath a strong veneer that I thought to be helpful, I suffered from both.

Living in Boston with Jon was perhaps not what he had envisioned. Changes in marital status do not change who we are. I sensed from his growing hostility this was a revelation for him. He perhaps was hoping the matrimony would give me a sense of security that would thwart my ambition. Yet in many ways, it only increased my passions.

My studies at Harvard quickly became an obsession along with my connection to a small group of students who were actively opposing the growing oppression in Eastern Europe. The steel wire fence we floated above had since been replaced with a twelve-foot cement structure. News of the atrocities behind the wall were now shared through underground reports, while a growing contingency of Germans living in America began to gather in the nearby pubs. In the following months, I feverishly planned to create and distribute a publication to assist in the efforts to free the people of Eastern Europe. I grew tall in what I thought was a valiant effort of justice and the perceived success of owning and operating one's own publication. Little did I know that my insatiable search to free others was ironically keeping me enslaved.

Emma's car pulled up the driveway, and moments later, I heard her in the yard. The lilt in her voice when speaking to the dogs now held a hint of sadness that lingered in the air with the smells of eucalyptus and pine. She knocked on the cottage door. "I'm back. We will need to leave here in about an hour."

I shoved the manuscript under the sheets. "Okay," I called.

She lingered at the door for moment before I heard the sound of her shoes pacing across the patio and vanishing into the house. I took a few deep breaths to slow down my racing heart, slid my hand under the sheets, and pulled back up the manuscript. I devoured the next chapter like a compelling novel. Emma's publication grew to a circulation of two hundred thousand and was distributed to educate Europeans on the sociology of freedom while uncovering leftist movements that were threatening democracy. *Your past is one you can never escape.* She wrote the line several years after starting the paper when a list of names from her underground contacts revealed that one of the leading members of the Red Army Faction, a terrorist group responsible for bombings, aircraft hijackings, and kidnappings was Emma's father.

The words took my breath away. I set the manuscript down. The thought that Sarah's death could be affiliated with Emma's father made me feel sick to my stomach.

Chapter 6

Our return from Vietnam was a media frenzy that led to Jon being elected to senator. Shortly after, I was appointed the US Ambassador to Germany. As grace would have it, I was now able to cross the East/West borders freely as I met with political leaders on either side, trying to dismantle the great wall of oppression I now associated with the atrocities of my father. This increased the pace and vigor in my life to the point where time now blurred.

Susan would no longer return my letters, and for this I did not blame her. There was a detachment in my prose that made every word feel disingenuous. How one can have such compassion for those unseen yet neglect the needs in one's own family remained incomprehensible to me, despite how well accustomed I had become to such an adaptation. Susan felt my preoccupation and retracted. I felt her anger and let her retract. Harsh words were never spoken. Silence became the knife that split the fibers of our kindred souls, and beneath the split lay a gaping hole of emptiness I clamored to avoid.

As days collapsed into months, a growing depression emerged. My energy began to decrease along with a swelling in my belly that I would come to know as Sarah. The pregnancy was as foreign to me as my first months in the States. Body changes and growing uncertainty as to my ability to care for such a vulnerable creation kept me buried in work until the day a warm current swept down my legs and a painful contraction sent me to my knees.

Sarah was delivered into my arms at a navy hospital in Western Germany. Her small, naked body was placed on my chest, and her brief cries turned into a quiet coo that attuned with a profound vibration in my soul. Jon came to our side the following day and had to return to the States by the weekend. Our relationship feeling the strain of our responsibilities while Sarah nursed at my breast, grounding me to the earth like a tree finally planted. In those following weeks, the warmth of her cooing and the sensation of warm milk flowing through my breasts melted me like warm butter on steaming bread. My heart opened with a seeping ache, and I fell in love in ways I did not know love could be, without concern for my own needs or desires, void of grasping or expectation, simple and undeniably safe. To love because the sheer existence of another depends on it is perhaps the purest form of love one can experience. It was a giving. And in that giving, I received my own maternal spirit. I received a life once again worth living.

SAN FRANCISCO WAS MORE THAN an hour away. Emma was still in pain, wincing with every bump, breathing heavily at times to manage the discomfort. I kept my eyes on the road, tilting the rear mirror so I could watch her as I drove. It was easy to imagine her at my age, her skin clear of the brown sun spots that dotted the sides of her face, her hair full with color cropped to her sturdy shoulders, falling onto a blue suit she wore to the embassy. She was far more successful than I would ever be but equally conflicted. Did it come with the age—the shallow ambition, the wanting to make a difference and the estrangement from loved ones that comes with the blind striving to prove you are worthy of something you already have?

I thought about David. Could it be that I found her memoir for a reason? Was it a sign to help me move closer to him or a calling to move closer to myself? I looked at her again, allowing her face to imprint in my mind. Every wrinkle told a story—lines that were not deep, like grooves in the sidewalk, but soft, like a thin leaf losing moisture. And I wondered how they softened after Sarah was murdered. How the anger and grief passed without leaving its indelible mark?

"Maybe we should stop somewhere and get your knee looked at."

"Oh, no … no. It's just a torn muscle. It will be fine by morning. Anyway, we have to meet Jake by 6:00 p.m." She opened a bottle of water and pulled out a pain reliever from her purse. "I think you are going to like him," she said. "He's been left by more women than God, but he sure has a good heart."

"Does he work for Oasis?"

"He's an escort for the children. He speaks Chinese, Vietnamese, and Thai, which makes him a wonderful resource in Asia."

I wanted to learn more about how Oasis was funded and how it was able to support so many children in boarding schools, but my questions were blocked, sidestepped, or completely ignored as we made our way through heavy traffic into the inner city. Cable cars now streamed through the streets. Lights on aging buildings, restaurants, and storefronts began to brighten while the sky dimmed to reddish-grey dusk.

"I think it's that next street," Emma said as I approached the stoplight.

"Where are we going again?"

"The Sansugo Restaurant. It's become too popular for my taste, but Jake loves the people there." Emma sat up and pointed over the steering wheel. "There it is, up this block on the corner."

We passed under the green lattice archways that marked the beginning of Chinatown, and I suddenly felt transported to Asia. Balcony banners with colorful oriental letters ran down the sides of four-story buildings. Traffic slowed to a near stop on the narrow streets, and we inched our way past sidewalks full of multinational pedestrians, open vegetable carts, and hanging raw chickens noosed on wooden racks behind storefront windows.

Emma pointed to an alley behind the restaurant. I dropped her off at the back entrance and parked. By the time I caught up to her, she was encircled at the bar by three men and a Chinese waiter attempting to tie a bag of ice around her knee.

"I've got the perfect cure for that swelling," said a tall, broad-shouldered Asian-looking man with moist, thin hair flattened against his forehead. "Lu, make Mrs. Davis an elephant seal," he yelled to the bartender before landing his eyes on mine.

"Jake, I'd like to introduce you to Kate, the woman I told you about."

He reached for my hand and lifted it toward his chest. My small fingers hid under my thumb as he looked into my face and bowed. "Can I get you a drink, young lady?"

"A glass of rice wine, please."

He smiled wide to expose a chipped front tooth while his eyes sparkled the way light bounces off water in a stream. The bartender slid a tall mug in front of Emma that smelled of warm cinnamon and buttery liquor. Emma swallowed a sip and then blinked several times while containing a cough. "I'm not going to ask what's in here," she said.

"Good. Just drink it. It's an old knee remedy."

"Then why is it call an elephant seal?"

"It's what elephant seals drink when they have swollen knees," he said with a grin.

Emma took a few more sips before limping behind a hostess toward a table in the front of the restaurant. Jake and I followed, as did a thin woman sitting at the bar who abruptly left her seat when Emma walked away. Two waiters and the Maître d' stood with open chairs, pouring water, delivering chopsticks wrapped in cloth napkins, and setting down hot appetizers I never heard ordered. On the adjacent wall, tall candles stood in bamboo holders with redwood dragons sitting like guards to a tomb. I sat down with Emma while Jake ordered her another elephant seal. The woman behind us moved to an adjacent table, her eyes flipping from Emma to her cell phone.

"Emma tells me you are from New York," Jake said in his loud, more-American-than-Asian voice.

"She's from Virginia. She works in New York. Right, Kate?"

"R—ight."

"Virginia. That is a big military state. Was your father in the navy?" Jake asked.

"No, he is a history professor."

"Asian history?"

"Mostly European."

"Asian history much more interesting."

Emma finished her drink, smiling at Jake in a way that made me think she wasn't really listening. If she had been, she probably would have had a thing or two to say about European history. The waiter brought her and Jake another elephant seal.

"Have you been to Asia?" Jake asked, pushing the drink in front of Emma.

I took a slow breath, thinking of all the times my parents had taken me to tour European museums. I had seen the royal jewels, spent days touring the Louvre, and walked into the lion cages of ancient coliseums but was embarrassed to admit I had never been to Asia. I shook my head.

"You need to take your father to Asia," he said. "Start in Beijing; go east to India and then west to Thailand. There you will see history. Real, ancient history."

A familiar voice came into the room as two men were escorted to the last open table across from ours. The man's New York accent echoed in my ears. I gazed over at him, and my breath caught. It was Michael, the intern from the *Journal*, being seated with a short, stocky man who I imagined to be his fraternity brother. My shoulders deflated with an exhale. *What's he doing here?* He looked at me, and I snapped my head toward Emma.

Jake smiled, waiting for a reply.

"I would enjoy going to Asia with my father," I said. "I'll talk to him about it when I get home." I looked over at Emma nursing her elephant seal while the thin woman in the table next to Michael stared at Emma.

"Emma tells me you are a writer?"

I leaned toward Jake. "I'm a journalist."

"A journalist. How interesting. You should write a story about how much money these women have contributed to save the lives of all those children."

"The money!" said Emma in a loud voice, which caused Michael and his friend to glance our way. "I have to give you the money." Emma raised her eyeglasses from the chain around her neck and rested them on the tip of her nose. She rummaged through her purse, the spectacles falling several times from her face before she pulled out a sealed envelope. "Here you go, good sir. Give that child a kiss on the head for me." She took a long sip out of the mug. "Going to school is the only duty a six-year-old should be required to do."

Jake pulled out a picture of the girl he was picking up, an Asian child with large, innocent eyes and raised red bug bites on her forehead and checks. Underneath the picture was a photo of a boy and girl who looked even younger. He explained that the local scouts in the region had identified these children as high-risk too. Their mother was an ailing prostitute infected with AIDS. When she dies, the little boy and girl will be turned over to his mother's master. They would then either be sold or enslaved by his organization.

Emma stared into her drink, circling her finger around the ring of the mug before lifting it again to her lips. Jake opened his wallet further and pulled out a stack of more photos—children he had picked up and transported to schools around the region. He handed me the stack. I thumbed through the photos with increasing reluctance before stopping on one that looked so familiar it pulled me away from my concerns about Michael. The child in the picture looked like me at her age. She had straight bangs across her forehead cut an inch above her eyebrows and a big gap between her two front teeth still growing into place. In her eyes shone the light of intelligence with an elusive sadness that shadowed beneath them.

"Where is this little girl from?" I asked.

"Cambodia. We lost her though. She was at the market with one of her teachers and two slave traders drove up and pulled her into a van. The athorties are still looking for her."

I looked back at the picture feeling weak, or maybe it was hopeless. There were so many people in Southeast Asia a child like her could be anywhere.

I shook my head. "It must be difficult to do this kind of work."

"Not really," he said. "Every person is a part of me and I am part of every person. When a child is injured we are all injured." Jake elaborated on a story about a little boy that soon trailed off in several loosely related directions. As I listened for him to return to the point, I realized how much I had kept myself in a bubble. In all of my years of journalism and the stories I covered on social issues in the Northeast region of America, I had not stumbled across an industry that was so profoundly damaging to human life. My neck began to ache from a tension pulling across my shoulders.

"These kids are more profitable than heroin," he said. "That's why the business is growing so rapidly."

"What do you mean?"

"You sell heroin once, and it's gone." He pulled out a picture of one of the little girls. "This child would have been prostituted hundreds, maybe thousands of times, and she would have never seen a dime of it."

My body continued to tense. I looked over at Emma sipping her drink. I wondered if this had something to do with the death of Sarah—if she had disturbed somebody's business transaction and the cost was her own child. My upper lip began to quiver, and I wanted to go outside for some fresh air.

"Excuse me?" The woman from across the room was standing next to our table with a martini in her hand. The dark circles under her eyes sagged into colorless cheeks as she stared at Emma. "Are you Emma Daines?"

Jake moved his hand toward the edge of the table.

"Yes. And you are?"

"Suzanne Andrews from the *Global News*. I was just researching an article on you. Do you mind if I sit down for a moment?"

Jake moved to the edge of the booth and stood up to block her from sitting. Two waiters rushed to his side.

"I just have a few questions about your daughter. Why have you never told the press who killed her? Who was responsible? People speculate that it might have been due to neglect or malice on the part of you or your husband. Is that the reason …"

"That's enough!" Jake said as he took the woman by the pit of her arm.

"Do you need some help?" asked Michael, who now stood at the front of our table. Jake and two of the waiters escorted the woman out of the building as she yelled back at Emma, still trying to get an interview.

"Hello, Kate," said Michael.

Emma looked up through the glasses sliding off the tip of her rosy nose. "Who is this nice young man?"

"I'm a …"

"He was on my flight. He is staying with his friend for the weekend. Come on, Michael. I really want to meet your friend." I grabbed him by the arm as Jake returned to the table.

"You didn't really get a job at *The New York Times*, did you?" Michael asked under his breath.

"We are still negotiating."

"Steven wants me to meet with Emma on Monday for an interview."

"Steven and I have a deal, and he has given me until next week to do the interview." I looked back at Emma, who was getting up from the table. "If you blow this, neither one of us is going to get the story." I nudged him toward his table, his friend looking at me with the leer of a bad come-on.

"You better hurry, then. Looks like they're leaving without you."

Jake was helping Emma put on her coat. I stepped back to the table.

"I used to like this restaurant," Emma remarked as she stepped backward, losing her balance before grabbing my arm. "Have I ever told you how much I dislike journalists?" she slurred.

"I can see why," I said.

She looked up at Jake. "You're right. That elephant drink made my knee feel better." Jake pulled up our car while we waited in the foggy air. A shiver ran through me, triggered more by shame than the chilled air. Being a journalist was like having a license to be intrusive. But if that was what it looked like, I wanted nothing more to do with it. I thought about how many times I had done something similar— waiting in bars and restaurants because I had a tip that the person I wanted to interview would soon be there. God, I hope I wasn't that obnoxious. Suzanne Andrews was a piranha looking for her next meal. There wasn't an ounce of empathy in her waif-looking body.

I took the wheel while Jake helped Emma into the car. A few turns from the parking lot, and we were back on the 101, heading south to Aptos.

Emma pushed her seat back with a long deep breath. "Why does everybody want to know about Sarah? My God, it's been over forty years, and they still want to know the same old dreary, God-forsaken details about my little girl." Emma's voice cracked. "You want to know why, Kate? Do you want to know why everybody is so interested in Sarah?"

"Why?"

"Because people love to hear about other people's pain. And do you know why?"

"No. Why?"

"Because they can't stand their own. They can't stand their own emptiness, their own mortality, their own feelings of rejection or unworthiness or shame that keep everybody running from themselves and toward everything that will never, ever solve their problems."

Emma looked up at the ceiling and reloaded with a deep breath. "It's what's wrong with this world, and it's why our evolution is going to get so ugly if we don't stop it." She yanked a tissue from out of the center dash and brought it to her nose. "You want to know what happened to Sarah, Kate? You want to know who killed her and how I felt about it? Do you want me to tell you the whole horrid, wretched story and what it did to my life? My husband's life? Our life together? Do you want me to tell you, Kate?"

I looked at the row of car lights beaming in my eyes. I did want to know. I wanted to know what happened to Sarah, and I wanted to know exactly how Emma felt about it. I wanted to feel her pain as badly as she did. And I wanted to know because I wanted to know Emma, not because I wanted a story for the paper. But I didn't want to know this way, not while alcohol was clouding her judgment. If I took advantage of her now, I'd be no better than the woman in the restaurant.

"No, Emma. I don't want to know. Maybe another time, if you decide you want to talk about it again."

"Sarah was a gift." Emma's voice crumbled into tears. "That's what you need to know, Kate. Not how Sarah died. Not how I felt about it. You need to know what I learned from her."

"I would like to know that. When you want to talk about it."

Emma rolled her head across the headrest and turned toward the window. A long silence filled the air. Then a light snore came from the corner of Emma's mouth. The opportunity to learn about Sarah had passed, and as it did, something inside of me started to bleed. I moved into the slow lane as my chest ached and then seemed to collapse with an anguish that had no words, tears, images, or sounds. I drove the rest of the way wondering who I was, what was important anymore, and what, if anything, I cared about. As the signs directed me toward Aptos, I began wishing I wasn't a journalist. I wished I never had to hear Steven's voice again or ask another probing question to exploit somebody's suffering or to cover up my own.

We pulled up to the house, and I helped Emma out of the car. She insisted on going into the kitchen to light a kettle for tea. Instead, we settled on a tall glass of water and two aspirin. I helped her back to her room, the dogs trailing behind, not quite sure what to make of Emma's condition. She ran her arm up the wall, flipping the light switch in the small master bedroom. As we walked in, I felt a sense of enchantment, as if I was entering into her nucleus.

Her bed was made with two tiers of pillows softening a pine wood frame with a rustic iron trim that curved in a floral design. Next to the bed was a nightstand with a small lamp, a stack of books tagged with markers, and a picture of her and Camille. Emma limped to the middle of the room and started to undress. I stood at the nightstand and set down a glass of water. "Do you need any help?" I asked.

"No, no, I might be an elephant seal with a liiii … tle tiny bit of a hurt knee, but I'm old enough to dress myself," she replied, folding her sweater into fourths before placing it on the top of a dresser, where she watched it slide off the edge to the floor.

"Everything has its place," she said. She slipped into a pair of faded blue pajamas with her husband's monogram on the sleeve. I watched her as if she were a child. There was a sense of strength in every wobbly move she made and a sense of vulnerability with every subtlety.

"I think we should prop your knee up for the night to keep the swelling down."

Emma snapped her head toward me, her long gray hair curling around her face in all directions. "Good idea, Kate Edwards. Good idea!"

I pulled down the covers, and she hopped on her good leg up into bed. I lifted her other leg onto the mattress, setting her swollen knee on top of a pillow.

"I brought your walking stick in. It's here by the bed if you need to get up during the night."

She smiled with her eyes closed and reached her hand up until she felt my face. Her boney fingers ran down my cheeks before falling onto her chest. "We have some things we still need to talk about," she said.

"Like why I am here?"

Her lip rose. "Maybe," she said before turning her face into the pillow to retire.

I squeezed her hand and pulled the white cotton sheet over her knee. "Good night," I whispered.

"You can sleep with the doggies in your room if you like," she whispered back. "They like you."

I turned off the light and closed the door behind me. Then I stood quietly for a moment to assure she was asleep. The dogs followed me into the kitchen. I lit the teapot and went out to my cabin to wash up and change. The cottage was cold, and I felt uneasy about staying in my room for the night. The concern of Emma waking up to go to the bathroom and her knee becoming too stiff or painful to move made me want to stay within a earshot of her room. I grabbed the quilt off the bed, threw her manuscript and the book she gave me in my bag, and headed back in the house. The teapot was just about to sing, the heat warming the kitchen from the brisk outdoors. With the quilt around my shoulders, I poured a steaming cup, walked into the living room, and settled into the overstuffed couch. The lamp on the side table cast a dim light, barely enough to read by, unobtrusive enough to melt my body into a state of ease. The night had brought Emma and I closer, and for the moment, that was enough. I set down my teacup and opened her memoir.

> The birth of Sarah changed our lives in unforeseen ways. Her brilliant smile and constant laughter brought a buoyancy to Jon and me that neither flight nor ecstasy could compare. She was angelic in all senses of the mortal word, and from the moment her light shined on my face, I knew that perhaps my greatest obligation was to not tamper with that which was divinely created. She came through me, not of me. She would have her own thoughts, her own soul, her own purpose in the world to discover. She was not to become what I was not or carry wounds that I could not burden. The patterns of my lineage and the sins of my father would need to rest with me to assure her a healthy life. For one …

"Kate?"

The sound of my name caught my breath, and my heart began to race. I looked up from the manuscript and saw the outline of Emma standing at the edge of the hall.

"Is that you?" she asked.

I pulled the manuscript under the quilt. "Yes, it's me."

"What are you doing?"

"Ahh … I was just reading. It was sort of cold in the cabin, and so I thought I would come inside for the night. I hope that's okay."

Emma turned toward the kitchen and then back toward the hall like a wobbly wooden doll holding a cane.

"I think I need some water," she said as she made a full circle and began to walk into the living room. I stood up and faced my back toward her as I tucked the manuscript under the red quilt and into the side of the couch. She plopped down into the wing back chair next to the fireplace and looked up at me. Her eyes were drooping along with the left side of her mouth. I reached down for her arm and helped her back up.

"Let's get you back to bed. I'll get you some water."

She flopped her arm around my shoulder and leaned into me. "What were you doing again?"

"I was reading. I wanted to make sure you were okay tonight."

"Why wouldn't I be okay?" she asked with a lilt.

"No reason, Emma. No reason at all."

Chapter 7

THE MORNING WAS CRISP AND still with the sounds of raccoons running up the tree trunks and the low jingle of Max's dog tag as he lumbered across the yard. I came to my cottage at the break of dawn and was able to sleep for another hour. It had been a quiet night after putting Emma back to bed. Instead of picking up her manuscript, I wrote. I couldn't deny that something was changing inside of me. As much as I wanted my life to remain the same, there seemed to be larger forces at play that had a different agenda. The thought of losing David from these changes filled me with fear. The thought of losing my dad seemed unbearable. I shook off what seemed to be ineffable and got up to brush my teeth. For now, I needed to stay in the moment and focus on Emma and how I could help her.

The kitchen was as cold as the outdoors when I entered, and there was no sign that Emma had been up. I set my laptop on the table and put on a pot of coffee. I was still in my cotton pajamas from the night before. The dogs sat beside the stove, their eyes following my every move until it occurred to me that what they wanted was food. I walked out to the patio and poured a cup of pellets into their bowl, hoping Emma would hear the food hit the metal pan and give me some kind of sign that she had made it through the night and could still walk on her knee. A shiver ran up my spine from the brisk morning air, and I hurried back into the house and shut the door.

Despite the cold, the stillness in the house was comforting. There was something about being in Emma's space that made me feel at home, or maybe it was the feeling of being less alone. I turned on my computer and sat at the table that was being washed by morning light, the sun beaming onto my back, warming the chill. A small trickle of mail popped into my inbox. Just a few weeks ago, my inbox would fill with more than thirty e-mails at a time. Today it was nothing more than a few reminders of press events I no longer attended and an e-mail from David. I got up and poured a cup of coffee and then sat back down and opened his message.

> Hey Babe,
>
> It's snowing here, and the city looks more like Christmas than spring. The apartment is cold without you. Hope this time away is giving you the clarity you need. When you come home, I'd like us to set the wedding date. I don't want to be on hold any longer. I know you understand.
>
> I love you,
> David

My small fingers tucked around the warm cup, rolling into my palm for comfort the way they did when I had to make decisions that made my stomach feel like I had swallowed a beehive. David was my safety net. He kept me from the edge, and I knew he would always catch me if I fell. I couldn't imagine being without him. But with him, I felt crippled. I was Kate the claw, and he was my protector, always rushing in to pick up even the lightest of objects or scanning the parties we would attend to see where I was, making sure I was near.

I ran my fingers through my hair and took a deep breath. *Why does this decision frighten me so much?* A sip of coffee ran down my throat as a door to the back bedroom cracked open. The sound of worn slippers slid across the brick floor until Emma appeared in the doorway. She stopped, gave me a perplexed look, and then headed for the coffee.

"Good morning," I said.

Her glasses were resting on the bridge of her nose, her long grey hair free-flowing down her back like the tail of a mare. "On a good morning, one is hiking by now. On a bad morning, I stay in my slippers."

I closed the lid on my computer.

"What happened last night?" she asked.

"How's your knee?"

She looked down and shook her leg. "It's still there. Doesn't seem as stiff today."

"Good, maybe that elephant seal really helped."

"Elephant seal?"

"That's the drink Jake was buying for you last night."

"Oh, yes. No wonder that man can't keep a wife. A drink like that will make you forget who you're married to. Did we get him the money?"

"We did. He is leaving this morning to meet with the girl's family, and the school in northern Thailand is ready for her arrival."

"Good. I'm afraid with this earthquake, we are going to lose the chance to pick up that little girl in Mexico. I'd hate to lose another one right now."

Despite her hangover, Emma's tone held the same passion as Camille's, the same sense of urgency, as if the deeper bond between them was crafted by this bold mission to save a small raindrop of enslaved children.

"I fed the dogs this morning. I hope that's okay."

"Thank you. They are not used to me sleeping in." She looked down at my laptop in front of me. "Have you been following the earthquake?"

"Not really."

"I can't imagine the *Journal* doesn't want to send you down there, since you are so close." She gave me a look of bewilderment before the cell phone in her pocket began to vibrate.

"Finally. Where have you been? I've left you two messages already." I could hear Camille's voice coming from the phone. Emma stood against the counter and looked at me.

"That doesn't mean he is hurt."

The rapid voice spilled from the receiver. The one-way conversation continued while Emma tapped her index finger against the corner of her lip. "Give it a few more days. Jess is smart. He will get himself out of there." Emma went silent for several minutes. "Tell Marie the same thing I'm telling you, and ask her to come over here tonight. We will have dinner and figure something out. Okay. I'll call you in a few hours."

Emma clicked off the phone and took a long, deep breath. Looking out the garden window, her gaze waned the way it did when she was deep in thought. Then as if she nudged herself, she pushed her shoulders back and looked at me. "Jess's fiancée is starting to panic. It's beginning to unnerve Camille."

I looked down at my closed laptop. While Marie was frightened to lose her fiancé, I was afraid to answer mine. My mother's voice emerged in my mind like background noise. *Just make a decision, Kate, and stick to it. The rest will work itself out.* I never cared much for my mother's advice. Then again, she had at least appeared to be happy with my father for the past thirty-five years, despite how much she traveled—or maybe because of it.

Emma limped over to the bread and slowly pushed down the toaster, as if she couldn't bear to hear the click when it engaged. "When did you say you were getting married?" she asked.

"We haven't set a date yet."

"Oh, yes. I remember now." She lifted her coffee cup as if it held a vague thought. "Wasn't there a man last night in the restaurant who knew you? And a reporter was there, too? A woman?"

"Yes."

"Reporters never cease to amaze me," she said. She stared out the window and then put down her coffee and went into the alcove. Drawers opened and closed before she reappeared. I was hoping she would return with the white envelope with my name on it. Instead, she tossed down a thin brochure.

"A friend of mine is putting on this retreat today. I think we'll head up there this morning." She took a sip of her coffee. "Can you be ready in an hour?"

"Sure, what are we going to do there?"

"I'm not sure. But I have a hunch she can help you figure out why you are reluctant to get married."

"Is she the silver maker?"

She smiled and tipped her coffee mug. "She's the one." Emma stood up and reached for the back door. "Come on, doggies," she said as she walked out to the patio. I watched her stretch in the yard for a few minutes, her slow motions becoming more fluid until she looked as if she was part of the landscape. The flow of her limbs was like branches gently moving in a breeze. She bowed at the end of what must have been a routine and then walked across the stone pavers into the cottage she used for an office. I let out a long exhale. *Thank God I deleted the message from Steven.*

I opened the brochure with a healthy dose of skepticism. It promoted the retreat as a weekend of self-discovery for women in business. From the first glance, it made me bristle with thoughts of group chanting and cathartic outbursts from strangers you were to treat like soul mates for the weekend. It was nothing I would have signed up to do for myself unless there was a story involved. And as I continued to read, I realized that the story would have been about the facilitator. Lynn Spears was a psychologist who left a private practice in San Francisco to become a leadership coach in corporate America. According to her brochure, she assisted executives in global organizations to manage the rapid changes, volatility, and personal obstacles they faced in the workplace. She was also the mother of two NFL players, which made me think her coaching had begun long before she made it her career.

～✦～

Big Creek Basin was a redwood forest marked by open meadows and lavish campgrounds, often used as a retreat center for Silicon Valley companies. The west side of the park rolled toward the ocean with low marshlands separating it from the sand. The trees beyond the marsh were as tall as New York buildings circling together to block out the sun.

The drive to Big Creek had been stone-cold quiet. There was no humming from Emma, pointing out historical sites, or clicking through the radio channels to hear the latest news about the quake. She carried an air about her I had not felt. She had not made eye contact with me since she walked out of the cottage office.

"So where are we going again?" I asked to push through the silence.

"You'll see in a minute."

A heaviness grew in my chest, and I began to feel like I did in the fourth grade. The day my mom found out I lied to her about a grade on a math test. I had been out sick the week before and didn't know the material. Sweating through the exam, I somehow came to the conclusion that failure was going to feel worse than copying the answers from the boy next to me. We both received a D, and when my mother found out, she seethed in a quiet withdrawal. As the acids churned in my stomach, I was starting to wonder what Emma knew and if the fourth-grade lesson wasn't coming back to haunt me.

The muddy road opened to a grass campground where a small crowd of women gathered around a fire pit. Just beyond them was an obstacle course that was built between two redwood trees. The tree to the right had a ladder of sticks that led midway up the trunk to a small wooden platform. Off the platform was a narrow horizontal beam that stretched fifty feet or so to a smaller landing on the other side. The sight of the ladder and the height of the beam made my head swim. My mouth went dry as my fingernails dove into the skin on my palms. *God, I hope she doesn't want me to climb that tree.*

Emma lifted herself out of the car and waved to a tall woman I recognized from the brochure. She walked with less of a limp to the fire pit, where she greeted her friend with a hug. Lynn smiled wide and authentic, like she was from the Midwest, and she was built just as sturdy. Her black spandex warm-up jacket stood at the collar to meet her short red hair that held a style despite the light mist. Standing next to Lynn was the only man in the crowd, a kind of wooly guy who resembled a bear in long shorts and V-neck T-shirt. He was working with another woman to help secure her into a body harness.

"I didn't think you'd make it," Lynn said.

"I'm surprised you weren't rained out," Emma said.

"Are you kidding? The rain just makes it more fun. Right, ladies?" The eight or more women around the campfire just looked at her, most of them rolling their eyes. "How is Camille doing?" Lynn asked.

"She still hasn't heard anything directly from Jess. A scrambled text was sent yesterday. But she's hanging in there. She has her candles lit."

"Oh, I'm sorry," Emma said as she turned back toward me. "Lynn, this is Kate."

Lynn reached out her left hand, the same way Camille had when we met, removing the awkward moment of shaking with my right. I nodded, my shoulders tensing toward my ears as I looked up at the beam. "I'm glad you could join us."

"Is this some sort of a camp?" I asked.

"A boot camp," one of the women around the fire said.

"It's not a boot camp," Lynn replied.

"Yes it is," said a few of the women in unison.

Lynn directed the man to help the woman in the harness up to the ladder. In his hands, he held the end of a rope that rose through

PAGE

a pulley on a cable that ran between the trunks of the two redwood trees. The cable was ten feet above the beam and appeared to catch the person if she fell. The other side of the rope was clipped onto the back of the body harness attached to a woman with feathered black hair who was as large as the man standing next to her with the rope.

"What you are looking at is a ropes course," Lynn said. "The woman climbing the tree is about to walk across that log." The narrow log looked to be about fifty feet in the air and spanned the distance between two redwood trees with landing boards mounted to the trunk.

"Is this some kind of a fitness program?"

She looked up at the woman. "Jan, do you mind if I share your story?"

"Go ahead. I'm going to die up here anyway," the woman said as she began to climb up the side of the tree.

Lynn leaned closer to me, gesturing with her hands as she spoke. She told me Jan was an executive for a software development company and had recently become overwhelmed with her life and frequently ill. She had difficulty saying no to people, and with the growth of her family and the company, she was finding life increasingly difficult to manage. The obstacle course, Lynn explained, was a way to help people manage their fears and behaviors that were counterproductive.

"How will this help her?"

She pointed up to Jan. "Watch."

Jan was now standing on the landing with her back against the tree as she looked at the narrow log. She slowly walked out to grab the two wooden rails before stepping down onto the log to make the midair crossing. She put her toe on the beam and then yanked her leg back.

"You can do it!" Lynn yelled. "Phil is here to catch you if you fall."

"Phil, you better not let go of that rope!" Jan yelled again.

"I've got you."

"I think I hate you, Lynn," Jan yelled back, putting her toe on the log again like she was immersing it into boiling water.

Lynn started to laugh. "It's okay to hate me. Remember, the rails are what you grasp for comfort."

Jan stepped back onto the landing and then approached the log again. Lynn kept a steady eye on her while explaining to me that the obstacle stimulates a person's fear response. Heightening the fears of a pattern allows the person to become aware of the thoughts behind the emotions. "Our fears are often attached to limiting beliefs, and those beliefs inhibit us from knowing what we are really capable of doing."

Emma looked over at me and then quickly turned away. Her eyes now held a hint of anger, or suspiciousness, or maybe it was betrayal. It was difficult to tell what was going on behind her tall, stoic pose and her aging face that only gave half an expression. A familiar sense of shame rose in my body. She must have somehow found out that I lost my job.

"Excuse me, are you Emma Daines?" a woman asked as she tapped her from behind. Emma turned to greet the woman while Lynn redirected my attention to Jan, who stood with one foot planted on the log as she held tightly onto the rails.

"I'm letting go now," Jan yelled.

"Of what?"

"My sanity!"

Lynn started to laugh. "What happens if you let go of saying yes to everybody and walk across that log?"

"I will let people down or disappoint them. Then I'll fall off this damn log and die!"

"And what if you do let people down or disappoint them?"

"Then they will see that I'm really not good enough to be in this position," she yelled as if the admission was giving her power.

Lynn turned to me. "This is fairly common, especially among women."

Jan placed her other foot on the log and stood up. She released one hand from the rail as her right leg began to wobble. She grabbed the rail again and sat down on the landing.

"Think about it for a minute. You can do this!" Lynn yelled, keeping her eye on Jan while she explained that the obstacle course was teaching her how to tolerate the physical discomfort of her emotions. "If we can observe our feelings and not act on them, we can make better choices. Like saying no even when it's uncomfortable."

I turned back to look for Emma. She was talking to a group around the fire. Lynn continued to explain to me about managing emotions while I struggled to contain the emotions in me. *Did Emma bring me here to climb this tree? Is this how she thinks I'm going to understand my fears about getting married—or is this some kind of Emma Daines hazing to see if I am worthy enough to write her story?* Anger rose, edging out my anxiety. I looked up at the log Jan was about to walk across, and my chest suddenly felt like the bear man was standing on it.

"How do you know Emma?" I blurted out to Lynn.

"Oh, we go way back. We did a future study project for Apple back in the eighties. She was brilliant. Her predictions came true. We've been great friends ever since."

Emma walked back to Lynn. "It doesn't look like your client is enjoying herself up there."

Lynn looked up at the landing. "Okay, Jan, time to start your walk."

Jan stood up again and placed one foot behind the other on the log. One hand at a time, she released the rails. Several moments passed before Lynn told her to take a step. She slid one foot a few inches ahead while holding her arms straight out from her sides. A gush of wind rustled through the trees, as she began to lose her balance.

"No way!" she screamed as she stepped back, grabbed the rails, and pulled herself onto the landing. "I'm not doing this!"

"It's only fear. Walk through it. Think about what's on the other side."

"I don't care what's on the other side. I'm getting down." She reached for the rails on the ladder and starting climbing down the tree.

Lynn turned to me. "See how powerful fear is?"

Emma stared at me with a gaze that held a thousand thoughts. "Do you want to try it?" she asked.

I held her eye contact through the long pause. The terror of being up that high made my head want to explode. But I felt I was being challenged and that whatever had made her angry might be overcome if I proved I could conquer a fear. "I would," I said, "but I think these other women are waiting for their turns."

"It doesn't look like anybody is in any hurry. Besides, it might help give you some clarity."

I looked up at the log again, my knees feeling like they were melting into joints without bones. A knot formed in the center of my throat; then an image of the little girl on the plane came into my mind. As the sun broke through a cloud and onto my back, I remembered her giving me the picture she drew. We were holding hands, standing on the top branch with wide smiling faces. *See, you're not afraid to climb trees anymore.* I turned to Lynn and nodded.

"Ladies, do any of you mind if we give Kate a try?"

"She can take my turn!"

"No, give her mine. She's a lot younger than I am."

"We've got time for everybody," Jan said.

Lynn put her arm around my shoulder and walked me over to the tree. "You don't have to do this if you don't want."

"No. It's okay. I can do it." I tucked my arms into a vest and strapped on the harness. Every cell in my body was on high alert, fully dreading what was about to happen next. On the back of the vest was a clip where the rope to the V-shaped line was attached. A snap that sounded like the slamming of a coffin rang in my ears while Phil clipped on the rope. My mouth dried like spit on burning asphalt, and my tongue felt like it was cemented to the roof of my mouth.

"Is there a situation in your life right now where you feel stuck or is somehow holding you back?"

I nodded, only partially hearing what she said.

"When you get up to the top, think about how you can move forward and the fears that keep you stuck."

"And what's the point of this again?"

"You'll figure that out when you're up there," she said as she patted my shoulder and gave Phil a nod to pull the slack out of the rope.

"I would feel better about this if I knew you, Phil."

"No, you wouldn't."

"Great. My life is in the hands of a funny man," I muttered under my breath as my fingers began to twitch.

I walked up to the base of the redwood and began my climb. My two fingers gripped onto the rungs of the ladder as I pulled myself up the first few steps. *Just look ahead*, I thought. *Keep your eyes on the tree. There is a big swimming pool down below. Nothing can hurt you.* The blood in my legs felt like it had rushed to my stomach. My inner thighs trembled as I pulled myself onto another rung on the ladder.

"You're doing great, Kate!" Lynn yelled. "Keep climbing!"

You're not going to fall. Just keep climbing. Why am I doing this? Damn it. I kept my nose close to the bark, and my eyes focused on the tree. An ant that was clearly smarter than me was making its way down while I looked up to the next rung. Another voice came from below as the sounds around me amplified—the crackling of bark as my knee rubbed against it, the breeze as it darted around the tree trunk, and the sound of my rapid breath as I sensed the distance from the ground. I looked down at the grass below, and my head began to spin. *How did I get myself into this?* The ladder led a few feet past the bottom of a wood platform. I reached the top and hugged the tree, frozen around its trunk like a child clinging to the legs of her mother. *You can do this. Emma's watching you. They are all watching you. Let go of the trunk.* I looked at the cable that led from the pulley to the back of my vest and then slid my body off the tree and onto the wooden plank.

"Great job! You made it!" Lynn yelled.

My back was pushed up against the trunk of the tree. I gazed at the beam, and my eyes shut like a cramped muscle. The picture the little girl drew came back into my mind. *You're not afraid to climb trees.* I took a deep breath and opened my eyes.

"As soon as you are ready, Kate!" Lynn yelled.

My mind went blank as I crouched down on the end of the plank. My arms wrapped around the wooden posts, hoping the tight grip would make the forest stop spinning. *Breathe into your belly. Deep into your belly.* The thought emerged as if the intense fear invoked a calmer, perhaps wiser part of me into consciousness. I sat down on the plank and rested my feet across the beam. My tennis shoes were no more equipped for hiking than for walking across a ten-inch-wide piece of wood fifty feet from the forest floor. I took another deep breath.

"Those rails are your security. They represent whatever you hang on to that keeps you from moving forward!" Lynn yelled.

I wrapped my arms around the smooth wooden rails. Looking down gave me vertigo; looking forward gripped my body with terror while the voice in my head continued to soothe me. *You can do this.* My arms tightened around the rails, and my palms began to sweat.

"Name the rails!" Lynn yelled from below.

I looked down at the rails and felt David's strong, lean arms. His strength, for a moment, passed through my body.

"O ... kay, I ... um. I'm ... 'm ready."

My toes gripped through my shoes as if they could somehow burrow through the hard wood. I took a deep breath into my belly. The voice in my head sounded more like my own. *There is a rope on a pulley. Phil is a strong guy. They must have insurance companies that determine this is safe. What if they don't have insurance? What if Phil gets distracted? What if the rope or the pulley breaks?* My heart now pounded through my ears, and my neck broke out in a red-hot itch.

"Are you ready, Kate?" Lynn yelled from the ground.

I gazed down to see if Emma was watching and got dizzy before I could spot her.

"When you're ready, let go, and move forward."

I wrapped my arm around one rail as I feverishly scratched my neck. The height, the fall, the look of the narrow beam registered in my mind as such extreme danger that it felt impossible to cross. I held onto the rails and felt David. The thought of letting go, of leaving the secure platform, was now so terrifying that my hands began to shake.

"You can do it, Kate! Visualize what you want on the face of the other tree," Lynn yelled.

I looked across the beam to the tree on the other side. *What do I want? What is worth risking my life for?* My hands steadied on the rails, and a silence emerged inside of me. I stared at the tree for several moments, and then an image appeared in the center of my mind like a film running across the inside of my forehead. I could see myself writing at a computer, absorbed in the material, feeling alive with passion. Beside me was a child, and then another. A sense of love came over me. I looked for David in the image, and a man in the background appeared. The muscles in my legs strengthened, and my chest bellowed with energy. I stood up on the beam. I wanted the life I saw in the vision. I wanted to be happy again—to love others and to feel a sense of purpose for what I was doing. And I was willing to walk through my fear to get it.

"Take your time," Lynn said. "Whenever you are ready."

I aligned my right foot in front of the left. The vision disappeared, and I stepped back and hugged the rails. *What if the man isn't David? How could I let go of him? He seems like the only person that could really love me.* I shook my head. *It doesn't matter.* Emma was watching; I had to make it to the other side. I looked at the tree across the obstacle and the vision reappeared. My strength came back and I leaned forward again.

I have a harness. The rope will catch me if I fall. I took a small step and let go of the right rail, my arm waving in the air until I found my balance. Then one trembling finger at a time, I released the other side. My heart pounded faster as I raised my arm toward the sky. I took another deep breath, and a step, and then another. I took three more small steps out on the beam, and it happened—the way you hear it happens just before you die. The forest went still. The world came to a complete and utter halt, and I entered a state of focused concentration that made everything underneath me disappear. My thighs firmed as if they were being infused with oxygen, and then a warm flow of energy rose from my belly to my chest that straightened my body and set my shoulders back. I took another step toward the vision. It suddenly felt so close and so real. I was free and about to be happy. I took another step, and before I knew it, I was too far out on the beam to turn back. I looked down for Emma, and my legs began to weaken. I lost my focus. *Don't fall … don't fall … don't fall.* Thoughts now rocketed through my head like stones thrown from a crowd. *Don't let her see you fall.* I moved a step forward, and my thighs began to shake. Both arms began to swing in the air. *Damn it.* I bent my knees for balance and came to a dead stop. My body was numb, paralyzed.

"It's okay, Kate. Stay with it! You're almost across." Lynn's voice sounded faint and far away.

Trust yourself. Trust yourself. What are you walking toward? The image struggled to appear, and then panic rose from my chest and wiped it away.

Trust the rope. Trust your legs. You can do this. I slid my right foot forward on the beam and suddenly felt off-kilter. The blood rushed out of my knees, and I was too weak to maintain my balance. My arms swung up and down, desperate to either gain control or take flight. The right side of my body tilted out beyond what I could balance. The world moved in slow motion as gravity pulled my shoulder toward the forest floor. I let go. A fleeting moment of total surrender—and suddenly, I felt the sharp tug of the rope against my back. The vest tightened against my chest and jerked me up into the air. Phil held me suspended as I swung below the beam, toward the trees then back again, relieved, angry, confused. Gravity pulled me to earth while Phil guided me to the floor.

Lynn walked up to me and pulled the rope loose. "You okay?"

"I think so." I choked back a flood of tears and then looked over at Emma. She was back by the fire, on her cell phone. Did she even watch? Did she see how far I made it across the beam?

Lynn put her arm around me. "She was with you the entire way," she said.

I looked back at Emma and then down at the ground, the tingle of adrenaline still vibrating through my skin. Lynn unfastened the harness.

"So what happened for you up there? Were you able to name the rails?"

"They were the arms of my fiancé, David." I spoke as if I had no filters, my thoughts spilling from their usual containers. "I don't want to leave him ... but with him ... I feel weak. Like I can't have what I really want."

"And what do you really want?" Lynn asked.

I thought about the vision, not sure what it meant, only recalling how alive it made me feel. "I'm not sure," I said.

Emma walked up and stood next to Lynn. Her arms rested in her jacket pockets. "You ready to get out of here?" she asked.

I nodded and hugged Lynn goodbye. Tears fell from my eyes as she pulled me into the kind of embrace that made me feel I had just accomplished something significant—even if it was terrifying. When Lynn let go, I turned and looked for Emma. She was walking toward the car. I stood in the cold, staring at the back of her head. I had passed her hazing. She could have at least congratulated me. Beneath the surface, tears of anger arose that made my top lip quiver. Emma stepped into the driver's seat. She was still aloof, and I no longer cared. In that moment, I hated her for making me climb up that tree, for inviting me to her house, for being alive in the first place.

Chapter 8

"I think the two of us should get a cup of coffee somewhere." Emma's tone sounded much like my mother's, with a stern edge that cloaked all semblance of warmth when she would return from a business trip to a report from my best friend's mother about how we missed curfew or smelled like cigarettes. Or the time we drank Peppermint Schnapps like it was water and ended up vomiting as if we had the Ebola virus in the bathroom at Taco Bell.

We pulled off the coast highway to a small set of gift shops that meandered across a bluff. My hands were still shaking from the walk across the beam as my seething anger toward Emma pushed up against her aura of suspicion. Neither one of us spoke as Emma led the way along a brick pathway to a patio dotted with white canvas umbrellas that overlooked the ocean. "Coffee or tea?" she asked in a slightly lighter voice.

"Tea will be fine."

Emma walked into the coffee shop. I sat down at one on the rustic wood tables and pulled my sleeves around my fingers to get warm. The coastal fog was beginning to burn off, and the sounds of otters playing below echoed off the steep, jagged cliffs. I stared out over the ocean, my mind shifting from thoughts of Emma to a pang in my chest to be back with David. I wanted to feel safe again in his arms, back on the sturdy plank where I knew I was okay, where life was predictable and my fears more manageable.

"Here you go." Emma placed a steaming teacup on the table in front of me and lowered herself into the opposing chair. Her green eyes that mirrored the deep currents of the sea looked at me over the glasses that rested on the tip of her nose. "We probably need to talk about a few things."

"All right."

"Before we left this morning, I went into my office. It looks like somebody had been in there."

My stomach dropped while I strained to hold my shoulders up.

"I invited you to my home because I wanted to know you. But what I need to know is, did you come to meet me? Or did you come to see if you could get the story about Sarah?"

I maintained eye contact with her without a blink. "I am a journalist. So yes, the story about what happened to your daughter did interest me."

"But is that why you came?"

"No. I came because you invited me."

"Do you know why I invited you?"

"Apparently you want an article written for the *Journal*." Even as I said it, I knew there had to be more. Emma was so well-known she could write her own story and any paper in the country would publish it. She didn't need me. Her hands began to tremble as she put down her coffee cup. She turned away to wipe a welling tear from the corner of her eye.

"Were you looking in my office for information?"

"No."

"Why were you in there?"

"I went in to use the phone."

"Why didn't you use the phone in the house?"

Checkmate. I felt like a child caught in a lie. I looked into my teacup and took a deep breath. Then my eyes rose to meet hers and my shoulders pulled back to straighten my spine. "I guess I was curious about what the cottage office looked like."

She squinted, her eyes focusing deeper into mine. "Did you look at any papers or go through my drawers when you were there?"

"No."

"Are you sure?"

"Yes. I only went in to use the phone."

She looked out to the ocean, then her shoulders released downward and she exhaled. "Who did you call?"

"The managing editor at the *Journal*."

She bowed her head and nodded. There was a long silence before she spoke. "I'm sorry," she said. "I've been harassed for such a long time now. It's hard to know who to trust anymore."

"I'm sorry, too. I should not have gone into your office." I held my tea with both hands. We sat quietly for several moments in a state of sadness—shared, unspoken sadness.

A flock of birds passed overhead. I wanted to fly with them—get home without being exposed and embarrassed for the pathetic lies that made me feel I had abandoned myself. It was in that moment that I wished I would have had the courage to tell her the truth. All the thoughts were there, and the words sounded reasonable in my mind; yet nothing came out of my mouth. I sat quietly, paralyzed by an ache, an intense fear that she was about to reject me that made no sense to me as I felt it. She was just a woman, an imperfect person, like me—a woman I didn't even know three days ago.

She looked at my small hand and then at me. "We all have a wound," she said with a sadness that deepened her tone. "We all have something that has hurt us deeply, that makes us feel rejected, or too inadequate to be loved. This wound over time can start to define us. But when we feel it, instead of run from it, we begin to recognize that it's not really who we are. It's what we fear we are." She looked out to sea, her hands no longer trembling as she took a drink of her coffee.

"I would like you, along with a few other people, to help me spread a message, Kate. We are spending too much time and resources running from ourselves, from our wounds, and we can't afford it any longer. We are about to evolve in a very significant way. All the signs are there, but we need people to participate in their own healing, allow their wounds and misconceptions to heal so they don't stand in the way of the gifts they have to offer. We need people to participate. It's the only way we will evolve safely."

I sat back in my chair, staring at the fine lines in her gold-toned skin, the softness of her gray hair, and the deep compassion in her eyes. I knew what she was talking about. My father had been telling me the same thing for years. "We are racing toward an apex," he would say to me. It's what history professors and sociologists seemed to know.

"Why do you need me?"

"Because you are young, and you're smart. People listen to their peers, and fewer and fewer people are in my peer group."

"I think most people at any age will listen to you," I said, looking into her eyes.

"Thank you. But I don't have the strength or the desire to do this alone. I need some trusted writers to help."

I cringed and looked away, my fingers pulling into my hand.

Emma looked down at her watch and then back at me. "There is something I learned from Sarah," she said, "something you need to know. I want to talk to you about that tonight. Lynn and Camille are coming over for dinner, but they shouldn't stay late." She took another sip of her coffee and looked at me softly. I nodded, my chest full of emotions I couldn't name.

"Did the ropes course help you with your wedding dilemma?"

The change of subject brought me a breath of relief.

"I'm not sure. I think I need a little time to think about what happened up there."

She gave me a blushing smile, tilted her head toward the sky, and then looked back at me.

"I have the perfect place for that back at the house. Grab your tea, and let's go." She handed me the keys. "Here, I think you should drive."

It felt like we had avoided a head-on collision. A sense of peace I didn't deserve filled the car as we drove back to the house. The dogs were lying on the front porch when we arrived. Max ran to my side of the car, and Sadie went to Emma's. She reached down and picked up the little dog, allowing it to lick the moisture off her lips while she pushed her head back and smiled.

"Come on, doggies. Let's go to the spa," she said.

Sadie wiggled out of her arms and took off running, leading us through the white lattice arch, past the cottages, and up a path made of smooth river rock stepping stones. At the top of the long walkway, through a line of tall trees, the path opened to a redwood bathhouse with bowed wooden beams that gave it an Oriental feel. Around the small house was an open deck where a lounge chair with a thick white cushion sat next to an empty hot tub set into the redwood patio. The back of the tub had a large wooden plug protruding from a copper spigot.

"A natural hot spring runs under the bathhouse," Emma said. "If you pull the cork, the tub will fill in about twenty minutes."

I walked out on the deck and inhaled. The smell of tall grass and lavender rose from the rolling hills below the deck, filling my senses. In the distance, the sun was making its descent toward the ocean, and the trees around the bathhouse stood tall and still in the cooling afternoon air.

"This is beautiful," I said. "So peaceful."

"I thought you would like it." Emma showed me the shower and pointed out the changing room with a built-in shelf filled with towels and a set of thick white robes.

I looked around, thinking about David. He loved to unwind in open spaces that were far removed from busy streets and steel glass buildings. "Can I ask you something?" I asked.

"Of course."

"How did you know your husband was the right one for you?"

She unfolded a towel and handed it to me. "I didn't. And I probably married him for the wrong reasons."

"But it seemed like you were so much in love."

"I was in love—or at least, that's what it felt like."

"Then why was it for the wrong reasons?"

"I was looking for something he couldn't give me."

"What were you looking for?"

She tilted her held and held my gaze as if she was remembering what she once felt like. "Safety. A love that wouldn't leave. And one that wouldn't constrict me, either."

"Didn't he give you that?"

She smiled and looked down with a blush. "Actually, he did. But back then, I was more focused on protecting myself against being rejected by him, or engulfed, rather than loving well." Her eyes came back to mine. "Camille has helped me a great deal in that regard."

"How's that?"

"She taught me that love is something you give to others, not something that can be taken from you. It's a verb, not a noun."

I looked at her, letting her words seep into my chest like a revelation.

She opened one of the cabinets and handed me a white canvas bag. "You should go get some clothes and whatever else you need and spend some time here. I'm going to check in with Camille and get ready for tonight."

"Can I help you with anything?"

"Oh, no. Just come on in the house around seven o'clock. That should give you a couple of hours to relax."

"Thank you, Emma. This is perfect."

She smiled back, holding eye contact as if she was looking for something inside me she couldn't quite find or wasn't sure she saw.

We walked back to the house. I filled a large thermos of water and put a fresh pair of sweats and a sweater in the canvas bag. As I walked out of the cabin, I noticed the corner of Emma's memoir protruding from the sheets. I moved toward the door and then turned around. There were a few hours to kill before dinner. That cushy lounge chair was the perfect place to read. Feeling empowered by the walk across the beam, I tossed the book in my bag and headed up to the tub.

There was no wind on the deck. The cork plug in the spigot pulled out with little effort, and a rapid flow of steaming water began filling the tub. Letting the smells of lavender and eucalyptus fill my lungs, I slipped out of my clothes and put on the cotton robe. Emma had left a towel over the back of the teak lounge chair and a blanket at the foot of the white canvas cushion. I set down my bag and curled my toes under the blanket. A white wide-winged bird with a long neck glided over the tub and then landed on the branch of a redwood. *If only I could cut through resistance so gracefully,* I thought, remembering what it felt like to be at the top of the beam. The safe yet uneasy feeling of being with David came over me like a chill. For years, I had waited for that discomfort to go away. I wanted to somehow find peace in the decision to marry, like a virtue of maturing or slipping into deeper love, or perhaps a form of acceptance that was just around the corner. Yet every corner led to another, and my life with him felt like walking in a maze with no exit.

I took a deep breath, closed my eyes, and turned my face to the sun. Warm rays wiped away my thoughts, exposing a sense of unease. I still had to find a way to talk to Emma about my job. She said she wanted to speak to me after dinner tonight. *I'll tell her then.* My breath deepened as I reached for my book bag, and pulled out Emma's memoir.

> My love for Sarah made family important. I wished most deeply to introduce Sarah to my sister in hopes that perhaps this common kinship would once again bring us together. Yet my attempts to contact her were met with silence, a mirroring of younger days when my

career and ambitions kept us parted like ships moving through seas of a different hemisphere. One cannot make it through life without certain regrets, and perhaps the greatest of these was the day I missed her small country wedding to attend a birthday celebration for the English Prime Minister. As the famous dignitary shook my hand, my sister's husband was taking hers. Later that year, Susan wrote to thank me for the wedding gift. Her tone of disappointment was so palpable that I distanced myself even further. If I couldn't be the sister she needed, perhaps it was best I didn't see her at all.

A light wind blew up from the hillside, and I pulled the robe tighter around my body. For everything Emma had accomplished, there seemed to be an equal measure of sadness. The distancing she described scratched at something inside of me. Was I protecting myself in some similar fashion, and would I someday hold the same regrets? I thought about my dad and the space his illness was creating between us, neither one of us wanting to deal with what was simply a matter of time. I looked down at the book. Emma's sadness was becoming mine. It was welling up in me and ready to burst. I turned the page and kept reading.

In the coming years, the logic that justified my separation from Susan broke down. It was a week, as some weeks are, when the beckoning of the soul rose above the perpetual clamor of everyday life. Sarah was fighting an insidious fever that left me feeling increasingly vulnerable and once again anguished by what is out of one's control. Her warm body was lying in my arms, her blue eyes reaching out to mine for relief, until the fever broke in the early morning hours. Sarah slept while I wept away the illusion of my independence. In the frail moments of life, when uncertainty aches through every bone, one can no longer deny the interdependency of the human spirit. Our soul's need for each other—to love and be loved, to live—is immense.

I wrote Susan again that morning. How little I knew that by the time I would hear from her, my life would change in a way that would challenge me beyond what seems possible to bear.

A splash hit the deck as the tub began to spill over. I sat the book down on the lounge and corked the pipe from the hot springs. The bath house was secluded by land and trees, so I took off my robe and submerged my naked body in the steaming water. My feet and hands tingled as the blood ran to my extremities. The long scrapes down my arms from the slide down the trail began stinging in ways that made me feel that I was healing. I cupped my hand with water and washed it over my face; then I slid back in the tub and rested my head on the edge. My eyes began to close.

Click, click, shudder, click. The white bird flew from the tree. *Click, click, click.* What was that? *Click, click.* I sat up in the tub and looked around. To the left of bathhouse was a man with a long-lens camera pointed at me. *Click, click, click.*

"Hey!" I yelled. "Stop that!" The man wearing a white V-neck shirt and a backward black baseball cap walked toward me, his camera still in hand, ready to shoot.

"I said stop! Come any closer, and I'll scream."

He stopped far enough away that I could get a head start back to the house, close enough to see dark hair sprouting up his chest and a dog leash draping from his shoulder. He let the camera drop around his neck and raised his hands above his head. Not far from him was a Golden Retriever who took off in a full sprint toward the bathhouse.

"Franky, get back here!" he yelled at the gangly-limbed dog. "Franky, no, no! Get back here!" The dog ignored his commands like a puppy running for chow as he ran up the side steps to the deck. His paws loped like oversized shoes as he stretched out his front legs and dove into the hot tub. I screamed and then screamed again. Water splashed into my eyes as the dog paddled in place. The man suddenly appeared on the deck.

"Franky!" he yelled as his eyes met my bare breasts. "Oh, no. Damn. I'm so sorry," he said as he quickly turned his back toward me, keeping his hands in the air. "Franky, get out of there!"

The dog jumped out of the tub and onto the lounge chair. I grab my robe from the side of the pool, stepped out while he kept his back turned, and wrapped it around my body.

"Franky, get over here!" the man said as he lunged toward the lounge chair with a leash. "I am so sorry about this. I didn't mean to scare you, and I swear I wasn't taking pictures of you." I stared at him while he was leashing the dog. His long-sleeved shirt was pushed up to his elbows, exposing a tattoo of a wild buffalo stampeding up his arm. He slid the camera around to his back.

"Hi again. I really can explain all of this. With the exception of Franky, here, who can't seem to stay out of anything that looks like a duck pond."

I kept my hands in my pockets and looked into his eyes, wondering where we had met. It's Matt. The guy that dropped off the script from Emma's interview. "Matt? You look so different."

"Oh ... I shaved. I let the hair on my face grow when I'm working on a project, and when it's finished, I shave it all off. I really didn't mean to scare you," he said, pulling the dripping dog from the chair.

"Oh, shit!" I lunged toward the cushion. The cover of Emma's memoir was immersed in a pool of water that was soaking into the pages. I grabbed the manuscript and started shaking off the water. "Damn ... damn ... damn ... I knew I shouldn't have brought this here." I wrapped the book in the robe in a frivolous attempt to restore it.

"Oh ... God ... I'm so sorry," Matt said as he handed me a towel. "I promise I'll get you another one."

"I don't know if there is another one." My eyes began to well. I sat down on the lounge and rested my forehead on the wet manuscript, my eyes finally giving way to a streaming rain of tears.

"Oh, it's okay. Really, I can fix it," Matt said as he stepped toward me and then rushed back into the bathhouse and returned with two clean dry towels. He placed one on my lap and used the other to towel off each page of the book.

"Maybe there is a blow dryer inside," he said as my tears gave way to a wail of emotion.

"Damn it. Emma is going to hate me."

"She's not going to hate you. It's just a bunch of papers."

"You don't understand. She invited me here to write an article for the *Journal,* and I don't work there anymore." I let out another cry and started to ramble. "I broke her chair in the cottage where I'm staying, and then I found this manuscript that I shouldn't have been reading in the first place. Then we took a hike, and I slipped into her knee, and she's been limping ever since. Now this." I lifted up the soggy stack of papers. A rattle of whimpers reduced me to a child.

"Hey, hey, it's going to be okay. I promise. It's not your fault. It's mine for not having Franky on a leash. I'm the one to blame," he said as he stood at the end of the chair. "I'll tell Emma it was all my fault."

Franky sat on the deck next to Matt, both looking at me with big, sincere eyes. I took a deep breath.

"Why were you up here taking pictures, anyway?"

"It's for my documentary. The Esalen Indians use to live in this region, and we think from some of the artifacts that they lived on this vista. I talked to Emma last week, and she said to come up and take pictures anytime. I forgot she had a houseguest."

"I was a houseguest. I'm not sure I will be after this."

He leaned toward me. "I'm sure you will be. Emma only asks special people to stay with her."

I looked down, feeling the complete opposite of special.

"I'm really sorry about the manuscript. I'm sure Emma will understand."

"What makes you so sure about that?"

"I've known Emma most of my life. We all hung out together."

"You hang out with Emma?"

"I don't really hang out with Emma. She and Camille cook for me, Jess, and her son, Tai, when we're all in town. She helped me with the research for the documentary, and once she took me flying with her."

"She has a plane?"

"She used to. Tai crashed it when he overshot the runway. Keeps telling everybody she is going to get another one, but haven't seen it yet."

I peeled the wet pages back on her memoir. It was almost completely destroyed, with only a few dry pages toward the end. And I was just getting to the part about Sarah. I gritted my teeth and stared at the wet, panting dog.

Matt reached down and touched my hand. "Did you get hurt?"

"No, no, I'm sorry. It's just a birth defect," I said, tucking my hands under my armpit.

"My little sister has a birth defect kind of like that. Have you ever tried archery?"

"Archery? Like the Indians?"

"Or like the *Hunger Games*. Your thumb and index fingers are probably really strong. I bet you'd be great at it."

I nodded only because I had no idea how to answer him. He stood up to leave, and I suddenly felt like I didn't want him to. "What happened to the Esalen Indians?" I asked.

"Most of them got sick and died."

"From what?"

"Various things. There were so many sociological changes going on in the area, and it was taking them too far away from their natural states. We are going to start filming as soon as we get the script back from Emma. You are welcome to join us."

"I wish I could. I'm going back to New York on Monday."

"Maybe next time." He pushed down his sleeve and scratched Franky behind the ears. "Again, I'm so sorry about the dog and the book. Do you want me to follow you down and tell Emma what happened?"

"Oh, no, no, no … I'll figure out how to tell her."

"Okay. Well, Emma has my number if you need it. Come on, Franky! Let's leave this pretty lady in peace."

Franky jumped off the deck and started running down the hill. Matt jogged after him, holding his camera in one hand and the leash in the other. I watched him until he was out of sight, wishing David could be more of a free spirit like him.

I looked down and uncovered the book from the towel. My stomach knotted. Chapters were soaked together like a wet newspaper, the ink traveling in a blur down each page.

Chapter 9

THE DOGS' BARKING WOKE ME from a depressed slumber. A car door shut, and I heard Emma in the front yard greeting a woman who sounded like Camille. The sun must have long ago set, and the only light in the cottage was coming from the bathroom. My head felt as if a large rock had formed in the center of my brain. My body lay motionless, not wanting to move.

I slowly pulled myself to the edge of the bed and looked over at Emma's memoir fanned in front of the space heater. The pages wrinkled and expanded like bark curling away from the tree. *I should just leave now—explain everything I have done and catch the next flight out of town.* I flopped back on the bed, thinking about something David said. *What if there really is a reason for everything, and this was some kind of karmic revenge for reading something I shouldn't have been reading in the first place? And maybe I came here for the wrong reason, too.* The story about Sarah had been washed away. David was right. I should have left the idea alone and focused on what Emma wanted to talk about in the first place. I released a moan. I wanted to go home—further home than David, to my dad's voice soothing me with reason and the strong aura that wafted through the room when my mother was near.

The sound of shattered glass came from the house. I stood up and peered through the blinds that covered the small front window.

Silhouettes of Camille and Emma moved through the kitchen like skaters across ice. Emma moved to open a cabinet on the far wall and then back again toward Camille. She reached down toward the floor and then back to the center island where their shoulders merged into a single silhouette. Moments later, the two figures separated, and Emma, the larger of the two women, moved to a bar stool across from Camille. The energy between them emanated even from a distance. It was as if each of them made the other brighter. *That must be what it is like to have a soul mate,* I thought as I noticed the crickets chirping in the yard, and the ache in my head began to subside.

The travel clock next to the bed flipped to 7:15 p.m. as the sound of another car rolled across the gravel driveway. I peered back out the window. The ladies were still moving about the kitchen when Lynn entered the room, her joyful voice silencing the crickets. Emma rose to her feet, and the ladies exchanged long embraces that blurred the lines of their bodies.

I sat back down at the end of the bed, trying to prepare myself to go in for dinner. Emma was planning on talking with me after Camille and Lynn left. I was still committed to telling her then about my job. *If the conversation doesn't go well, I can get a room by the airport for the night and take a flight out in the morning.* I packed a few things into my suitcase and then lifted the book off the space heater. A few pages before the end of the book were still legible; other than that, it had been destroyed. I closed the cover of the manuscript and slid it in my book bag along with the book she had given me the first night I arrived. I probably should have read that instead. Reading about how people found their life purpose would have probably been more productive.

"Kate!" I heard Emma's voice call out the back door. "Come over for dinner whenever you're ready!"

I'd be ready in about twenty years. Until then, the best I could do was put on my big girl pants and hope that Camille and Lynn left early. There was no mirror in the cottage, which at this point was a blessing. I threw on a pair of clean jeans and a heavy knit sweater and followed the sound of Lynn's voice into the kitchen.

Emma saw me coming and pushed open the back door. Lynn and Camille were seated around a butcher block table, cutting vegetables and drinking red wine.

"Sit down," Camille said.

"Can I get you a glass of wine?" Emma asked.

"She's going to need one after today," Lynn said.

"The ropes course couldn't have been worse than the hike Emma took her on yesterday," said Camille as she tapped her long red fingernails against the face of her cell phone.

"Oh, I can imagine," Lynn said as she turned to Emma. "If there is a trail, she takes it, even if she has no idea where it's going to lead. If you are with her, you can be gone for days."

"I'm glad I didn't know that yesterday," I replied.

"I haven't lost anybody so far," Emma said as she raised her glass of tea.

The kitchen was warm and the room thick with a welcoming intimacy. I took a sip of red wine and felt my shoulders release and move down my body. Camille, wrapped in her long purple sweater, waved me over to sit next to her on the stool. Her body tilted next to mine as she held her hands toward the stove to get warm. Camille looked older than just a few days before. Her vibrant brown skin was now drained of energy like a bright flower wilting under the summer sun.

Lynn was her energetic opposite. Her face was round and strikingly cheerful with high cheekbones and milky white skin that was framed in thick auburn hair, chopped at her chin. Her lips were full and shone with color that added to the sparkle of her long chain necklaces and gold clanging bracelets.

"Have you heard any more from your son?" I asked Camille.

"No, but we got a call from the little girl's grandmother today. She wanted to know if we had picked her up."

"Is this the woman from Los Angeles?" Lynn asked.

Camille nodded and then explained that the little girl Jess went to escort to the boarding school was the child of a Protestant who lived just south of Tijuana. The woman struggled with an addiction issue and recently caught a boyfriend using her child for pornography. "Given her situation, she doesn't feel like she has the power to stop it, so she reached out to her mother, who is a housekeeper in Los Angeles, and together, they found Oasis."

"Is Jess picking up the girl from the mother?" Lynn asked.

"That was the plan. But the grandmother hasn't been able to get a hold of anybody in her family and fears that the child is missing or dead."

"What happens when you call Jess's cell phone?" Lynn asked.

"It goes straight to voice mail. If I don't get something more concrete by tomorrow, I'm going to drive down there."

Emma spun around from stirring her soup, not noticing the drops splattering off the wooden spoon onto her hand. She stared at Camille. "You are going to do what?"

"I'm going to go find him. He might be hurt, or stuck, or God knows what, but I'm not staying here any longer."

"Camille, the freeways are closed at the border. People can't just drive into the area," Lynn said.

"People can't, but mothers can. I'll find a way to get to him. He needs me. I can feel it."

"You stubborn woman," Emma said as she stirred the soup and shook her head.

"You would do the same thing."

"You're right. So I'm going with you."

Lynn and I stared at them as they stared at each other.

"Only if you have finished what you started," Camille said to Emma in a tone that could cut through bone.

"Don't start with me …"

"Emma, are you going to put some meat in this soup?" Lynn asked as she reached between them to grab the wine bottle. "Because if we are just eating vegetables, I'm going to order myself a roast. And you're going to pay for it."

Emma nodded at Camille. She pulled a bag of potatoes out of bowl and started to wash them in the sink. The tension in the air was now part of the comfort. Potato peels flew onto the floor, the dogs ran to eat them, and Lynn moved to add ingredients to the pot, catching each of our gazes for a silent check-in.

"You are not driving down there," Emma said.

"And how is that even remotely more dangerous than flying into Vietnam in the middle of the night?"

Emma glared at her, then back at her soup.

"And did I try to stop you?"

"Yes. You were ready to have me committed. And you probably should have," Emma said.

"But I didn't. And you went anyway. You found Jon even though the rest of us thought you were bat sick crazy"

"Bat sick crazy?" Lynn started to laugh. "I've never heard you talk like that before."

"What would you do if one of your sons was missing after an earthquake?" Camille said to Lynn.

The room went silent. The chopping of vegetables had reduced to the sound of a slow slice breaking through the fibers of a small red potato.

"Then it's settled," Lynn said. "We are all going to find Jess in the morning."

Emma tore the top leaves off a parsley sprig and tossed them one by one into the pot. "We are not settled yet," she said.

Lynn wrapped her arm around Camille's shoulders while Camille and Emma looked at each other as if they were holding a private conversation.

"What did you think of the ropes course today?" Lynn asked.

"It was definitely more challenging than it looks from the bottom," I replied. "How did the rest of the women do?"

"Two more made it across, and Jan tried again. All in all, it was a good day."

"I still don't understand why you do that to those women," Camille said. "Why does anybody need to get in touch with the fear of falling off a fifty-foot-high pole? Shouldn't you be teaching them how to get in touch with their kindness, or compassion, or something more useful?"

"Most of these women shut those feelings down a long time ago to try to make it in their careers."

"God knows I've done that before." Emma said as she pulled a set of gold cloth napkins from a drawer.

"I'll set the table," Camille said.

"No, you need to rest."

"I'm not tired. I'm just cold for some reason."

"Maybe you are coming down with something. God's way of telling you it's not a good idea to go to San Diego."

"A little cold is not going to keep me from finding Jess."

Emma shook her head and walked into the dining room with the silverware. She returned with a dark green blanket and draped it around Camille's shoulders. Camille and Lynn carried on a conversation about the ropes course that cast a thin veil over the anxiety about Jess. While they bantered back and forth, Emma remained quiet, her brow furrowed into deep pleats across her forehead.

The loud *ping* of a timer went off. Emma grabbed a red mitt and opened the oven door. A wave of heat filled the kitchen with the smell of warm sourdough bread. She lifted out the steaming loaf and slid it off the pan onto a cutting board. The women now worked in unison, as if they had done it a million times. Emma carried the bread to the table. Camille filled large bowls with the hot soup and topped it with fresh shredded cheese while Lynn poured the wine into the glasses on the rustic teak dining table adjacent to the inside garden. Emma ran the condiments to the table and waited until the rest of us were seated. She lit a three-wick candle in the center of a pinecone arrangement and took her seat next to Camille.

"What an unusual table," I said, rubbing my hand across the deep curves in the dark wood.

"It used to be the front door of a church in Bali," Emma said. "We found it on a trip to Indonesia one year when we went to pick up one of the girls. Remember the man who sold us the door?" she asked Camille. "He had such an insatiable crush on you, he offered to take it to America himself."

Camille smiled but didn't speak, her face growing a lighter shade of pale as the blanket cast a tint of green onto her moist skin.

"How long are you in town, Kate?" Lynn asked.

"I'm leaving tomorrow evening."

"Are you working next week?"

"Actually, I might take a little time off. I think I'm going to head up to see my parents for a few days."

The room went awkwardly quiet as spoons clanged against bowls. Lynn broke the silence with a story about a nonprofit endeavor, which started a discussion between her and Emma, while Camille leaned back and sank further into her chair.

Emma reached for Camille's hand. "Are you okay?"

"I'm fine. Just tired."

"Do you want to go lie down in my room? I can bring the soup back a little later."

"No. No. Really, I'm fine." She pushed back her shoulders and sat up in her seat.

The dancing flicker of the candles captured my gaze. My mind drifted in and out of the conversation while I daydreamed about the best way to tell Emma about my job and now her memoir. The thought crossed my mind to pack the damaged book and never mention it. But the raw ache of guilt that thought provoked eliminated it as a possibility. *If only I could get Camille alone,* I thought as I looked at her fading in her chair. *I could show her the memoir and ask her what to do*. I had come to admire Camille as much as Emma. Just being in the same room with her made me feel loved, and more at ease. There was no doubt she would know the best way to tell Emma, but I didn't want to disappoint her either, or give her reason to think that I had been snooping around to find information about Sarah. My eyes moved to Lynn. She was who I felt most connected to. Lynn was at least ten years younger than Camille, and something about the way she looked at me made me feel understood. How could I get her alone?

The conversation shifted in tone, and I tuned back in.

"I'm surprised he called, after what he put you through!" Emma said to Lynn.

"He is having a hard time with her illness."

"Is that hard on you?" Camille asked.

Lynn took a sip of wine and swallowed her bread like a fat pill. "We were married for twenty-five years. I'm going to be there for him if he needs me."

"But what about …"

"That doesn't matter. It was just his way of running. I can forgive him for that," she said. Her shoulders never moved from their upright position. If she tipped her head, she could carry a steel beam on those shoulders, and I was starting to think maybe she did. My eyes shifted from Lynn back to my soup as I thought about what it would be like if David left me for another woman. The idea came with a slight sense of relief. As much as I hated to face the truth, it was becoming clear that he wasn't the one for me.

"One of my clients just lost her job," Lynn said to change the subject. I darted my eyes around the table. "It would have been a perfect time for her to do the ropes course, but I couldn't get her to come to the event."

"Losing her job might be good for her," Emma said.

"She's not seeing it that way. Her identity was so tied to her role, she's completely lost right now."

"Does she have support?" Emma asked.

"She has a partner. But she doesn't really open up and connect with people. My sense is she doesn't want to be known. That's why the job was so important."

"Sounds like an invitation," Emma said, reaching for more bread.

"It could be."

"An invitation to what?" I asked.

"Don't get her started," Lynn said to me as she raised her glass of wine.

"You know it's true," Emma said.

"Yes, I do. And you need to write the book about it so I can give it to clients like her. But first you need to publish your memoir. That's an important story."

I choked on a gulp of wine and started to cough. I reached for a glass of water so fast I tipped over the full cup and it poured toward Emma. I jumped to my feet with a napkin.

"I'm so, so sorry," I said, reaching across the table to mop up the spill dripping into her lap.

"It's okay," Emma said. "It's just water."

Camille patted my arm. "It's really no big deal."

I sat down, trying to keep my composure while my chest sank into my belly. Just being in their presence made me feel exposed, like every thought I had was read more clearly than I could read it myself.

Emma placed her napkin over the water in her lap and continued. "The important story," she said, "is that this accelerated change we have been experiencing for the past sixty years is leading us into a transition. All of us are being invited to participate, but we have to understand how this change of consciousness comes to us and how to participate in the process of our own healing." She turned to me. "This is what I want you to write about, Kate. It's the most important thing happening to humanity right now. And it's only the beginning."

I looked up and caught Lynn staring at me. She looked away and back at Emma.

"But like you said," Lynn responded, "people have a choice, and not everybody chooses growth in situations like these."

"It's our responsibility to choose growth. If not, we will only add to what will become a very destructive future. And it does not have to be that way." Camille's face drained of color while Emma's passion rose and her voice deepened. She looked at me and raised her spoon. "This topic would make a great article for the *Journal*. Your demographic is full of professional women and men who can intuit the change in consciousness we are experiencing and want to participate."

My throat tightened, and the soup that had tasted so good was now bubbling from the acids in my stomach. *I don't work there anymore.* I wanted to blurt it out, yell it across the room, drop this heavy, wet veil, and hope the women in the room would still like me anyway.

"Excuse me," Camille said as she stood up from the table. "I'm feeling a little dizzy. Do you mind if I go lie down for a moment?"

"Are you okay?" Emma asked, reaching for her hand.

"Oh, I'll be fine. I think I'm just fighting a little bug. Sorry, ladies, you know I always hate to leave a lively conversation."

Camille's skin was now white and moist. Her hands slightly trembling as she put down her napkin. Emma moved the heavy dining chair and walked Camille down the hall. When the women were out of sight, Lynn put her napkin on the table and turned to me.

"So how long have you been out of a job?"

"How do you know?"

"It's written all over your face. Were you laid off?"

"Yes. About three weeks ago."

"I'm sorry. It's happening to some really good people right now."

"It doesn't feel that way. I think if I were as good a writer as Emma thinks I am, I'd still be at the *Journal*."

"Have you told her?"

"No. I haven't managed to get the words out of my month. And now she wants me to write an article in the *Journal*. I don't want to disappoint her. But every moment I'm here, it feels like I'm creating a bigger disappointment." Tears began to well in my eyes. I took a sip of water as a soft smile lit Lynn's face.

"You are not going to disappoint her," she said. "I can promise you that."

I rubbed away a tear that broke from the well.

"Is that what was going on with you on the ropes course?"

"That, and my life in general."

"When you were holding on to the rails, what did you imagine you were holding on to?"

I thought about being at the top of the platform, looking at the beam as if it were a bridge that needed to be crossed. "My fiancé, David. He has been so kind and protective of me that I have really wanted the relationship to work. I want to give him the wife he needs. But with him, I feel handicapped, or maybe less competent than I am, and he seems to prefer it that way. Being out here, challenging myself in the ways I have, has made me realize how smothering it has been. But it's also been very safe. Now that I lost my job, it's just seemed too frightening to let go of him too."

"But you did it. You stood up and walked. Do you remember what gave you the courage?"

"You mean besides not wanting to embarrass myself in front of a bunch of people I didn't know?"

"Yes, besides that."

I went back in my mind and thought about standing up on the log and the resistance I felt in every muscle. It all looked dangerous—the drop, and the log, and not knowing what it would be like to be out in the middle. Then I focused on the tree, and I saw a vision of the future for the first time in months. I could see myself writing again, but in a different way—a way that was much more fulfilling than anything I had ever known. "The idea that I could fall became less powerful than the vision of the future," I said. "That's when I started to walk."

"That sounds like a great conversation to have with Emma," she said while she poured me more wine.

Emma rushed into the dining room, putting her arms in a long black coat. "I need one of you to drive," she said.

"What's going on?" Lynn asked.

"Camille's having a difficult time breathing. We need to get her to the hospital."

"I can drive," I said.

"Good. Let's go."

We all fired on instinct. I ran to my cottage to grab my keys, anxiously threw a few things in my book bag, and ran out to the car. Lynn walked out the front door with a handful of jackets, tossed them onto the hood, and then quickly walked back to help Emma with Camille. They eased her down the porch stairs, holding her under each arm as they helped her into the back seat. I heard Camille's labored breathing as Emma wrapped the blanket around her and tucked her under her arm.

"We might need two cars," Lynn said as I stepped into the driver's seat. "Follow me. There's no hospital in Aptos. We'll have to take the freeway north to Santa Cruz."

Lynn jumped in her white sedan and raced out of the driveway. I pushed the pedal closer to the ground to keep up with her, not wanting the speed to be uncomfortable for Camille.

"I forgot my phone," Camille said while I turned the corner and flew down the hill.

I looked at Emma through the rearview mirror, and she mouthed the words, "Keep going."

"We can get that later," Emma said in a voice so deep it was comforting.

Camille winced. Then she winced again.

"It's okay," Emma said. "First, we need to get you to a doctor."

"You have to tell her," Camille said in a labored voice. "Promise me you will tell her."

"That's not important right now."

"Yes, it is," Camille said, her voice fading with her breath.

There were moment of silence then Emma let out a low moan.

"Camille...Camille." she said. "Damn. She's lost consciousness."

I looked in the rear view mirror and saw Camille's head limp on Emma's shoulder. "Hurry up, Kate. Please hurry!"

My hands began to shake on the wheel. My heartbeat pounded in my temples as my eyes focused on the back of Lynn's car. *Please help me get her to a doctor in time.* Emma needed Camille, and something inside of me was starting to need Emma. I turned on the emergency lights and raced to the hospital.

Chapter 10

The pinnacle of my career largely seemed like an unreal series of undeserving acclaims. Even my name became associated with a kind of prestige that felt as if I were watching another through a two-way mirror. It was here, at the top of what most would consider a lifetime of achievement, where I took my greatest fall. My sister Susan died suddenly that June; her husband's voice, a call I barely remember, echoed through my aging ears in such a way that I lost my equilibrium. I took to the floor in my room, the ebb and flow of grief intermingled with a distinct and pervasive summons. My soul was calling me home. The pull to return had such relentless vigor that it seemed no personal will, nor human act, could have changed my course.

This time of deep awakening drew me into the belly of great despair. It began with memories of holding my sister as a baby, playing with her cotton-soft hair, moments of delight colliding with a sense of utter shame like waves careening in a storm. My fears of inadequacy had divided us, rejecting the heart that was my own. My tears turned to sobs as I became her. I felt Susan's emptiness, the lost feeling of an abandoned child sentenced to a boarding school, her need for me, and the walls this created in her. I saw Jon's face and was pulled into the ecstasy of our lovemaking and then the rapid descent back to earth, where fear rose and the impulse to flee engulfed me. The image of my father then haunted me for days—the hatred he acted out on me, which in turn I had for myself. After a night of bitter exhaustion, I felt my body release him. The war I fought to counter the evil he perpetuated only served to keep him alive inside of me.

I SAT IN THE FAR right corner of the waiting room, curled in my chair so my legs blocked the damaged memoir from sight. It had been over an hour since we arrived at the hospital, and Emma and Lynn were still behind the white steel doors that lead to the emergency room. I looked over to the young man pacing the floor, the lean muscles on his arms bulging through his undersized t-shirt. A few rows behind him sat an older woman dozing over a pushcart full of empty bags and shredded sweaters. My gaze brought me back to the memoir. The handful of pages still legible at the end of the book made my chest ache with compassion for Emma. Her sister must have recently died, and now Camille was sick. Trying to keep my mind from racing with worry, I focused again on the remaining pages.

The following weeks were filled with memories, night sweats, and waves of abject emotion—my mother's face as she kissed me goodbye, the fresh smell of Sarah's skin as I tucked her into bed the night she vanished, the sight of Jon, at rest in his casket, decorated in a uniform that draped over his frail, cancer-ridden body. Emotions came and went with the steadiness of the tides, washing up and away deep-rooted feelings once visited yet not fully expressed.

In the final days of this spontaneous process, I could only tolerate water and light fruit. My cells, now empty, were preparing me to receive. At the end of the week, I was awakened by a full moon framed in the window of my bedroom. I sat up, alert, alive, summoned to a vision that projected across my eyes. The image of snakes intertwined, a universal symbol of God and man, gave way to an angelic vision of Sarah. Her golden skin, playful smile, and the flow of her curly hair beckoned me closer. In my mind, she took me through a warm passage, as if walking through an open artery in an immense organ. At the end of the passage, a thick flap opened, and I entered into a scene that appeared to be the heart of humanity—one organ made up of all beings. A deep, almost intolerable ache ballooned in my chest, and I became aware that I was experiencing a pain well beyond my own, a global suffering. It was the pain of a collective heart destroying itself under the influence of ignorance—of individual and collective self-protection.

I then saw a wall crumbling to the floor in my own heart, a barrier that once held my pain in and kept me from fully loving others. Susan, my mother, Sarah—they were all a part of me, still with me, waiting for me to realize that we are not separate, nor can we survive much longer under the illusion that we are. The breath of a great spirit filled my body and from here I realized, with the deepest sense of my being, that we can erect and dismantle the great walls of the world, but we will only truly survive as a species when we dedicate ourselves to removing the walls from within.

I was startled by a loud sneeze that came from the older woman hunched over her cart. She looked at me and then turned away. I stared into the water-damaged pages. This must be what Emma wanted to tell me about Sarah—not why or how she died, but what she represented to Emma today. I looked at the clock; another ten minutes had passed. My worry had oddly subsided, and I returned to finish the book.

It was only through such an inner journey that I was able to unite with my purpose and piece together the significance of my life. To my great delight, beyond the long days of grief, I would find that what I had learned throughout my career was abundantly relevant, yet only of meaning if applied to what was meaningful.

It is in the discovery of self-love and the abolishment of self-deceit that one finds inner peace and can at last bring what is most needed into the world. The source that brought me to such awareness revealed to me the significance of such a journey. It is only by way of our individual awakenings that the world will create the kind of change that is necessary for our survival. For that which is within is within us all, and that which is denied will manifest in our outer realities with increasing severity in our attempts to cleanse the bodies in which we all reside. This is to be the calling of all who are conscious.

The emergency room doors swung open. I closed the book and tossed it back in my book bag. Lynn and Emma entered the room. Emma's face was drawn, pale, and expressionless.

"Is she okay?" I asked.

"She's had a heart attack," Lynn said. "She's still unconscious, so it will be some time before they can assess the damage."

"The damage?"

"Her heart stopped. They're not sure for how long," Lynn said. "They are going to keep her in the intensive care unit for now. They said they will call us as soon as we can see her again."

Emma's arms wrapped around her shoulders, and her long black coat hung straight to her knees. She looked around the room filled with metal chairs, the pacing man, and the dark-haired woman now asleep again over her cart.

"There must be a chapel in this place," she said through a listless breath.

"I'm sure there is," I replied. "I'll help you find one."

Lynn went to the cafeteria in search of coffee while Emma and I walked the other way through the empty corridor of the small community hospital. A night janitor mopping the floor directed us to a worship room at the end of the hall. A chill ran through my bones, and I tucked my hands in my sweater to try to get warm.

"This must be it," Emma said as she turned the knob and pushed open the worn white door to a dimly lit room. Rows of dark wooden benches faced an arched stained glass window that was lit from behind. Illuminated in the beaded glass were three doves circling a full-body image of the Mother Mary. Her brilliant blue robe flowed from her shoulders, covering arms that were opened wide, reaching toward the birds. Beneath the glass was a narrow wood table holding candles on either end of a small metal cross. Emma stared up at the glass window, and I stepped up to her side. My hands hovered over the two flickering candles casting small rays of heat that added to the natural warmth of the room.

"This isn't how I thought this weekend would turn out," she said, looking up at Mary.

"I'm sure Camille is going to be okay."

She dropped her head and clasped her hands. "I'm not so sure, but whatever happens, Camille will make the best out of it. She always does, you know. She has a heart I wish more of us could have."

"Why's that?"

"She loves without fear. And she loves every moment of every day. It's what makes her so beautiful." Emma released a deep sigh. "Sorry," she said. "This probably is not what you expected when you came to California."

"I'm not sure what I expected. But right now, I'm glad I'm here."

"I'm glad you're here, too."

I followed Emma to the middle bench, and we took our seats in front of the makeshift altar.

She softly pressed down on my hand and then pulled out the rail to kneel. I sat in silence as she rested her arms on the back of the front bench and bowed. My mind was as still as the air that filled the room, while a silent language emerged between us that told me she needed to create her own space.

The stained glass window pulled me into its essence. I had seen images of Mary before, in churches and museums all through Europe, but none of them struck me the way this one did tonight. Her eyes were dimly lit, and the gold plates of stained glass encasing her head made her appear three-dimensional. I leaned into the bench, remembering my grandmother's funeral. My feet were in a pair of black patent leather shoes, dangling from the pew while I stared up at a statue of Mary. She towered over me with open arms and the energy of tall trees. My mother, deep in her own tears, shushed me when I asked who she was. A moment later, my father dipped his head and whispered in my ear, "She's a symbol of God." It was the only time I attended church with my parents. Yet the image of Mary and the words of my dad stayed with me, as did the feeling that she was always looking over me.

I opened my eyes to check on Emma. Her back rose and fell with a steady, deep breath as the ceiling began to creak with the sound of a hospital gurney wheeling across the top floor. I looked back at the light coming through the frame of the door and wondered what was holding Lynn up. My feet rubbed across the tile, curbing the urge to go find her, hoping I could catch her alone and show her the damaged manuscript and at the same time not wanting to leave Emma's side. As my thoughts raced, my connection to Mary faded. I suddenly felt enshrouded in my body, isolated by skin and bone, aware of every conflicting thought that kept me in turmoil.

Emma's head rose, and her hands pressed against the bench while she pushed herself back into her seat.

"Are you okay?" I asked.

She reached into her pocket, pulled out her cell phone, and checked the time. "I have never liked waiting for this kind of news," she said. "Seems like I have done this in my life all too often."

I nodded and remained quiet.

"How about you? Are you okay?"

"I'm fine. Do you think Lynn got lost?"

"If she's lost, it's only in conversation with somebody."

I smiled and thought about Camille, her labored breaths in the car and the words she spoke before losing consciousness. "Do you mind if I ask you something?"

"No, not at all. I have come to trust the intentions behind your questions," she said with a smile.

I nodded while releasing a deep breath. "When we got in the car, Camille said, 'You have to tell her.' Was she talking about me?"

Emma looked at me and then down into the Kleenex in her hand. "Yes, she was."

"What do you have to tell me?"

She inhaled deeply through her nose. "I don't really know where to start. I guess at the beginning." She turned toward me and rested her arm on the bench. "About six months ago, I received a call from my brother-in-law telling me my sister, Susan, had suddenly passed away. I went back to her memorial service in Virginia, and when I was leaving, her husband handed me a box of her things. In the box was an envelope that had a private adoption certificate in it. Apparently, Susan got pregnant in college. She didn't have the money or means to care for the child, so she put the baby up for adoption." Emma stopped, looked up at Mary, and then wiped a tear falling from the side of her eye. "I wish to God she would have told me. I could have helped her keep her baby." She took a deep breath and turned toward me. "The baby was a little girl that was adopted by Jean and Peter Stetson."

My head suddenly constricted as a hot flush came over my face. "Jean and Peter Stetson from Northfolk, Virginia?"

"Yes."

"My parents?"

Emma nodded.

My heart started to race. My small fingers shaking against my palm as my skin went numb.

"I don't understand."

Emma looked down into her napkin.

"But how can that be?" I asked. "My mother died the year after I was born."

Emma shook her head. "No, she didn't, Kate. Your birth mother was a nursery school teacher who lived in Elkwood, Virginia, and died seven months ago from a brain aneurysm."

I pushed my palms into the sides of my forehead, as if it could keep my head from exploding. My parents lied to me about my birth mother? She had been alive the entire time. I missed knowing her, or at least meeting her, by seven months. How was that possible?

"You're lying. They must be a different Stetson. There is no way."

Emma looked into my eyes, her focus now enveloping me. I stood up from the bench and moved away from her.

"Why didn't you tell me before I came?"

"I wasn't sure ..."

"You weren't sure of what?" The question hung in the air. "Why didn't you just tell me in a letter instead of putting on this charade that you wanted to get to know me?"

"It wasn't a charade. But I understand how it could have felt that way."

"Then what was it? A test? The hike. The ropes course. Was all of that to see if I was worthy enough to be your niece?"

I slammed my hand against the side of the bench, and a loud bang echoed through the room. Tears I was determined to hold back began streaming down my cheeks.

"I didn't know what your life was like, Kate. Or if this was going to be information that would be good for you. When you told me your mother died when you were a baby, I knew what this would do to you. I know you have good parents, and right now, your father is ill, and I wanted to be respectful. I didn't want to destroy or harm anything they had built for you."

"Destroy it? This annihilates it!"

Emma looked up at me and took a deep breath. "I'm sorry. I didn't know how to tell you."

"You lied to me!"

She looked down into her tissue and then back at me. "I was confused, and I very much wanted to know you for many well-intended reasons. But I didn't lie to you."

"You withheld the truth. It's the same thing." Feelings of betrayal ripped at my chest with so many origins that I couldn't begin to name them. I pushed against the bench and marched out the door.

My head felt like it was being crushed in a vise. I stormed past a janitor before running into Lynn with a tray full of coffee.

"Good news," she said. "Camille's vital signs are stable."

"Good," I said as my voice cracked, "because I have to leave."

I ignored her calls as I ran toward the parking lot. All I wanted was to go home and forget that I ever came to Aptos. My mind raced while I jumped in the car and started the engine. She had to be wrong. There were other Stetsons in the area. *Emma doesn't know who my parents are. She doesn't know me. She's a crazy old woman who takes hikes that don't have trails.* The wheels screeched out of the parking lot, and I headed toward the freeway. *They wouldn't have lied about something like that. Why would they lie?* I merged into the fast lane. *But what if it's true?* I shook my head. *No, it's not true.* My foot pressed into the gas pedal.

The lights from the oncoming cars were blinding when an ache I faintly knew rose in my heart. I could have known my birth mother. She lived in Elkwood, thirty minutes away from the house where I grew up. I could have seen what she looked like, heard her voice, maybe felt something I was never able to feel with my mother. *Stop.* My head began to turn from side to side. *Don't go there, Kate. This isn't true.* I looked at my watch. It was 3:00 a.m. on the East Coast. I wanted to call. But I couldn't. Not yet.

I missed the freeway exit to Aptos and had to circle back around. The road through town led me up the hill to the red mailbox. I let up on the gas pedal and turned onto the gravel road. Before I could stop the car, a pain pierced through my heart like a knife stab. I pulled into the roundabout and fell over the wheel, my tears turning to deep sobs as my body began to tremble. My foundation was cracking, crumbling, breaking open, and I was falling through it. My breath turned rapid and shallow. I want to go back to the way it was, before I knew this, before I knew Emma.

The dogs followed me through the side gate and into my cottage. They stood in the open doorway while I threw my suitcase on the bed and tossed in my clothes.

The envelope—the white envelope in Emma's desk with my name on it. *Damn.* I ran out of the cottage and threw my body into the warped wood door. The lights were on in the kitchen, and most of the food was still out on the counter. I stormed into the alcove and opened the desk drawer. The white envelope was still on top. I tore it open and pulled out the first of two documents.

Certificate of Live Birth
State of Virginia

1-87-40-003377

Name of Child—First   **Middle**   **Last**

       Michelle   Emma   Franks

Sex	**Order and Distinctions**	**Date of Birth**	**Hour**
F	Single birth; 7 lbs, 2 oz; 21 in	8-1-1972	18:03
	Underdeveloped fingers on right hand		

Place of Birth   **Street Address**

Memorial Hospital   3200 Hospital Way

                              Harrisonburg, Virginia

Name of Father   **Date of Birth**

Unknown   Unknown

Name of Mother   **Date of Birth**

Susan Marie Franks   3-10-1950

Physician or other attendant   **License number**

Dale E. Shapiro, M.D.   GO39883

The only information I recognized was my birthday and the distinctions. I turned to the other document—a certification of adoption that officially changed the baby's name to Katherine Jean and parents to Jean and Peter Stetson of North Folk, Virginia. Beneath their names was the street address where I was raised. The adoption date was three months after the live birth.

I ripped off my jacket and gripped my right hand, crushing it with my left like I was trying to kill the enemy. My head swooned and I dropped into the chair.

I turned over the birth certificate and looked for a seal or any evidence that it could have been a forgery. It was embossed with the hospital seal in the right-hand corner. My mind went blank. I was reduced to pure awareness, as I lost all sense of an identity.

The dogs began to bark, and a car rolled up in the driveway. My body sat, frozen stiff in the chair.

"Kate? Are you in here?" The heels from Lynn's shoes clicked across the floor. "Kate! There you are." She said as she walked up to the doorway of the alcove. "You have a few people worried about you back at the hospital."

I stared at her, feeling the hot flare of anger streaming from my eyes.

"Are you okay?" she asked.

"No, I'm not okay. There's nothing okay about this."

"Why don't we go sit in the living room?"

"No. The only place I'm going is home."

"I think we should talk about what happened tonight first."

"There's nothing to talk about. Emma misled me. She invites me out here, tells me she wants me to write a story for the *Journal*, and then dumps this landmine on me." I tossed the birth documents on the desk. "My parents clearly aren't who I thought they were. God knows what reason they had for telling me my mother died the year after I was born. And my birth mother, who apparently gave me up three months after I was born, lived thirty miles away from the house I grew up in and passed away seven months ago." I stared up at Lynn. "And my name isn't even Kate. My birth name is Michelle Emma Franks. Unbelievable!" I pressed my hands into my forehead.

Lynn pulled up a chair that was resting against an adjacent wall. "That is a lot to absorb in one evening," she said.

"I want to go home."

"I bet you do."

I started to cry, folding my arms across the desk and putting my head down facing the wall.

Lynn leaned against the doorway, still facing me. "I don't know if you can hear this right now, but we have known about you since Susan passed away last summer. Emma brought back those documents, and Camille tracked you down. Emma spent a great deal of time wondering and worrying whether reaching out to you was the right thing to do. She really wanted to know you. And because of the timing of things and the fact that you were a journalist, I think it made Emma believe that you might be part of the greater vision she sees."

"Then why didn't she just tell me that upfront?"

"Probably the same reason you didn't want to tell her you lost your job at the *Journal*."

"That's different."

"What makes it different?"

"I didn't tell her because I didn't want to be rejected."

"Maybe Emma didn't want to be rejected either."

My numbness faded. I suddenly felt naked with nothing to clothe me. "Is this really true?"

"That's for you to determine. A lot of truths have been taken from you in your life. To really know who you are, you will have to find your own answers."

I pulled the sleeve of my sweater over my hands. "Different name. Same deformed fingers." I let the words sink deep into my chest. "No!" I pounded on the desk and then stood up and moved away from Lynn. "Why would my parents lie to me?"

"I don't know. Maybe they feared that the truth would someday lead to their own rejection."

"Their rejection? The only person that got rejected here was me. From my fuckin' mother, because I didn't have ten perfect little fingers and toes."

"Is that what you think?"

I lifted my hand. "What the hell would you think?"

She stepped toward me, and I stepped back against the wall. "No. I do not need this right now," I said.

"What do you need?"

144

"A flight home." The thoughts in my brain contracted like I was in labor. "Home, wherever that is." *I can't believe my parents would lie to me.*

"Even intelligent, loving people can do some pretty crazy things when they fear they might be rejected."

"But lie to me and tell me my mother had died? That makes no sense."

"I know. It doesn't make sense to me either."

I picked up the adoption papers and sat down in the chair. *One stupid piece of information, and my whole life has changed.* I stared at words on a page. "Susan Franks was my birth mother?"

"It appears that way."

"And she was Emma's sister."

"Yes. And that makes you her only remaining blood relative."

"Damn it. Why didn't she tell me this sooner?"

"Why don't you ask Emma that question?"

"Because I hate her right now."

Lynn rested her hands on my shoulders. "You have a right to be mad—at several people."

Her touch was grounding. It brought me back to myself, and I started to cry. She pulled me into her arms and held me. Her long embrace was like a cocoon, swaying me as my mind melted into liquid, anger giving way to compassion, my thoughts reconfiguring into new realities. Several moments passed.

"What do you want to do?" Lynn asked, still holding me.

I opened my eyes and thought about Camille. "I guess we should go back to the hospital," I said.

"Good idea. I'll drive you."

We stood up and moved toward the door as a phone began to ring in the kitchen. It rang twice before we realized it was coming from Camille's cell. Lynn jumped to pick up the call.

"Hello? Jess, is that you?" Lynn said as her eyes widened and her chest bellowed. "Are you okay? Oh, does your mother ever need to hear your voice right now! Let me get to her and call you back. Okay. Call you soon."

"Let's go," Lynn said, and we raced out the door.

Chapter 11

WE HIT EVERY STOPLIGHT ON our way to the freeway. When we reached the on-ramp, Lynn pushed the gas pedal to the floor and maneuvered into the fast lane like an ice skater racing inward for position. My mind was speeding as quickly. I could know about my mother, a thought that lingered in my mind like an old cobweb in the corner, while ambition kept my sights looking forward. I wanted to know all the pieces now and find out as much as I could.

I looked down at my cell phone. My father always told me not to call people after 9:00 p.m. I wondered if that applied if the caller was your daughter who just found out her mother didn't really die a year after she was born. Knowing my parents, that wasn't enough to qualify. Emotional issues were best left until morning.

"Damn," Lynn said. I looked up to see a spiraling red light reflecting off the rearview mirror. She pulled off the freeway in the same manner that she entered and rolled down the shoulder to a stop.

"How do I look? Lynn asked as she fished through her purse.

"You're not serious," I said, looking back as a policewoman approached the car. "She's a woman anyway."

"Yeah, so, how do I look?"

"You look like a speeding ticket," I said while Lynn rolled down the window.

"Good evening, ladies," the officer said, flashing her light into the car. "You two in a hurry to get someplace tonight?"

"Our friend's in the hospital, and we need to get back …"

"Either one of you ladies been drinking this evening?"

Lynn snapped her head back to me. Her eyes grew wide as I stared at the red wine stains still on her teeth. I brushed my fingers across mine to warn her. She mouthed back, *Oh, shit.*

"We definitely had a glass with dinner," she said to the officer. "But that was a few hours ago."

"Can you please step out of the car?"

Lynn took a deep breath and handed me her cell phone. "Here," she said, "text Emma and tell her we are on our way."

Lynn and the officer walked toward the police car while I caught a glimpse of my reflection in the rear-view mirror—pale, smudged with mascara, lost in the vacancy of my own swollen eyes. I fell into the back of the seat. My birth mother was Susan Franks, a school teacher from Virginia. And Emma Daines was my aunt. My head shook from side to side. How could that be?

The police radio squawked through the misty cold night air. The officer wrote up a ticket as Lynn stood next to her. I looked at her cell phone and pulled up the last text from Emma. There were a series of messages between the two of them since I had arrived—Lynn asking Emma if she had told me yet, and Emma responding. *Her father is sick, this might not be the right time.* The reminder of my father's illness and the ineffability of his loss trumped all emotions. I exhaled and put the thought, with the feelings it caused, back in its compartment. I focused back on the phone and texted Emma. *Lynn and I are on our way back. See you soon.*

I reached down into my purse and pulled out Emma's memoir. The swollen pages fanned out from the spine. The book was now twice its original size, a mass of white fiber morphing into a new form. I turned on the overhead light and tried to find the pages where she wrote about Susan. My stomach was starving for something I couldn't taste. My heart felt like it was trying to reach out of my chest and grasp onto an image that was fading. The pages ripped from the center as I pulled them apart, flakes of fibers falling onto my dark sweater. There was nothing left about Emma's sister that was legible. Her description washed away with the ink. I set the book in my lap and thought about their escape from East Berlin, the two of them crashing down in the balloon and recovering in a farm house. Susan was only ten. How did she make a life for herself from there? I suddenly wanted to interview her—more than I ever wanted to interview anybody.

The car door opened, and Lynn jumped in. "Long gone are the days when I could talk my way out of a ticket." She tossed the yellow slip into the glove compartment and looked down at the manuscript. "Doing a little reading while you wait?"

"You could say that. It's Emma's memoir. I found it in my cottage the first night I got here."

"That's her memoir?"

"Unfortunately, I had a little run-in with a dog at the hot tub."

"My God. What does the *dog* look like?"

I looked at her and shook my head. "I shouldn't have been reading it in the first place. Now how am I going to explain this?"

"Right now, that book is the least of your worries."

I looked down at the book. "Actually, it's become a symbol for all of my worries."

"Did you read about Sarah?" Lynn asked as she sped up to enter the freeway.

"Only about how much she changed Emma's life. The book was destroyed before I got to any details about how she was killed or who killed her. Do you know?"

"Yes, I do. And I got to tell you, Emma is one remarkable woman to have survived that."

There was no reason to bother asking Lynn what happened. She wasn't about to betray Emma's confidence, and I wasn't about to insult her by asking.

We drove the rest of the way in silence while I wondered what I was going to say to Emma. I wasn't ready to apologize for calling her a liar. And I wasn't ready to be her niece. All I really wanted was to know about my mother. What was she like? What did she believe in? Did I look like her?

The tires screeched around the curve, and we pulled into the parking lot outside the emergency room entrance. Lynn jumped out of the car.

"You find Emma," she said. "I'll find out if they will let me see Camille."

I ran past the reception area and then turned down the hall and stopped. *What do I say to her?* I leaned up against the wall and looked up at the white stucco ceiling. My mind washed to a blank slate, and then a thought entered as if it was given to me. *Listen to her.* I took a deep breath and walked toward the small chapel. Emma was still sitting in the pew where I left her, her back against the bench with her head bowed. The sounds of my boots stepping across the hard tile echoed throughout the room. Emma turned when I reached the bench, her high cheekbones protruding from tired skin as our eyes met in a sweet sadness.

"Is it okay to sit here?"

"Of course," she said as she slid down the bench.

I sat down and pushed myself up against the corner of the seat. "Any news about Camille?" I asked.

"No, not yet."

"We got a call from Jess. He's just north of LA, on his way back. Lynn went to see if she could tell Camille."

Emma's head fell back, and she let out a long exhale. "I knew he was fine. But what a relief to hear it. Thank God."

I nodded and started rubbing my small hand. "I'm sorry about my reaction earlier. It was just a lot to absorb all at once."

"I'm sorry, too. I wish I could have found a better way to tell you."

We both looked up at Mary. The air was so still, I could hear the candles flicker. We sat through a long pause that didn't need to be filled, and then Emma started speaking like she was thinking out loud.

"Susan's husband called me last June to tell me she had passed away. It was so sudden and shocking. I guess when you have a younger sister, you always think you will go first." She shook her head and looked up at Mary. "That logic has failed me before, but not like this. When I heard she died, I was paralyzed with regret. I had been so preoccupied with my own life that I hadn't paid attention to hers." Her eyes dropped down into her lap as she pulled apart small edges of her tissue. "I made mistakes with Susan. I always thought that things between us would eventually work out—that someday, when the time was right, we would have the conversation we needed to have and repair the old wounds. But time ran out." She looked at me with her half-moon smile.

"After the funeral, her husband handed me a box of her things, and in them was an envelope with your adoption papers. It was the first time I found out she had been pregnant. It just broke my heart that she didn't feel close enough to me to tell me."

Every muscle in my body felt tense, like something painful had just hit me, and something more painful was about to. I looked up at Mary. "Do you know why she gave me up?"

"Apparently she got pregnant with you in college. She thought she would be able to raise you on her own, but shortly after the birth, she became debilitated by depression."

"Depression?"

"We had a tough childhood, Kate. I can only imagine all the things she was going through. She wasn't responding to medication, so after a few months, it sounds like a couple of social workers convinced her to give you up for adoption. She was married a few years later and was never able to get pregnant again."

"It wasn't because of my fingers?"

Emma slid toward me and placed her smooth, bony hands around my deformed one. She looked into my eyes. "No, Kate. She wanted you. And knowing Susan, she loved you very much. She would have done what she felt was the best thing for you over the best thing for her. I promise you, this sweet, beautiful hand of yours had nothing to do with it."

My brain hurt, like it was suddenly reversing its orbit. Tears began to move down my face in a steady stream. "What was she like?"

Emma held me with a soft gaze. "She looked just like you. She was quiet, and shy, and loyal, and so very loving. After our mother died, I would tuck Susan into bed each night. We used to sleep in these small boxes in the cellar that were not much bigger than a drawer. She would wait, sometimes for hours, until I turned off the light and went to bed, and then she would crawl in next to me and fall asleep under my arm. I would hold her so tight. Just feeling her breathe made me feel more alive."

"She sounds very sweet."

"She was a very good person. One of the best. And you know what else about her?"

"What?"

"She loved to write."

"She did?"

"Yes, she did. And she knew how to write in several different languages."

A feeling of wholeness, or maybe it was strength, was starting to form in my chest. It was as if a distant part of me had finally returned. My spine grew tall, and I took a breath that felt connected to me, to a wiser or perhaps more mature spirit inside of me. Emma looked up at the stained glass window. The thinning skin around her eyes was now unpleated and smooth. "There is so much about your mother I wish I did know."

We sat in silence. Emma was holding my hand with both of hers, resting the ball of entwined fingers in the cushion of her warm underbelly. "You were right," she said. "I should have told you earlier. I wasn't trying to mislead you; I just wasn't sure if telling you was what was best for you—or for your family. When you told me your father was ill and you believed your mother died when you were a baby, I wasn't sure what to do anymore. Camille kept insisting that you needed to know, but I didn't want to do the wrong thing for the wrong reasons."

"Camille was right. I did need to know."

She squeezed my hand. The warmth in our little cocoon was softening the skin on my fingers. "I'm sorry I didn't stay closer to her," Emma said. "When I found out about you, it somehow felt like maybe Susan was giving me another chance. But those are the dreams of hopeless romantics and old fools like me. I know better." Emma shook her head and smiled as if she was laughing at herself. "Sometimes we put desperate pieces together and create the wrong picture," she said.

"Maybe it wasn't the wrong picture."

She shook her head. "I'm ashamed to say there were some self-serving assumptions. When Camille found you and she told me you were a writer, it suddenly made sense to me that you would be part of this project. Then once I met you and I learned more about your life, how good your parents have been to you, and the family you have back home, I realized I was being foolish." She looked down and then met my eyes again. "That was part of my hesitation too. I feared that I was painting a picture that was best for me and perhaps not at all what you need or want." She released my hand and clasped her own. "You have to follow your own path, not mine. And I'm old enough to know that I should not try to persuade you, or anybody, otherwise."

The tension in my body was gone. All I could do was stare through the open space in my mind while the deeper parts of me continued to reconfigure. We sat quietly for several moments, looking at the rising light shining though the stained glass window, allowing the pixels that defined our relationship to shift in silence. I felt a slow warmth rise in my chest.

"So you're my aunt?"

"I hope at this point that's not a disappointment."

"No. It's not." I turned toward her and rested my arm on the back of the bench. "But I have a couple of confessions to make that hopefully won't make me a disappointment to you."

"I doubt that," she said.

I rolled back my shoulders and held her gaze. "A week after I received your invitation, I lost my job. I was afraid if I told you, you wouldn't want me to come, and I really did want to meet you."

Emma cocked her head to the side, looking at me as she nodded.

"I'm sorry. I no longer work at the *Journal*."

"That explains a few things," she said, "but it wouldn't have mattered. You are still a great writer."

"I had no way of knowing it wouldn't have mattered. And I guess my self-serving desires were getting the better of me, too."

"You not working at the *Journal* does not make you a disappointment at all," she said.

"There's more …" My stomach tensed as I reached into my book bag and pulled out the destroyed manuscript. "The night I got here, I found this in my cottage. I know I shouldn't have been reading it. My curiosity got the better of me."

Emma's face went blank. Her eyes shifted onto the clump of swollen pages.

"I only read the first couple of chapters. Then I took it up to the hot tub with me, and it got wet."

She reached out her hand, and I gave her the manuscript. She placed it into her lap, opened the cover, and thumbed through the chafing paper. Her breath appeared to stop. Then she turned it over and looked at me.

"I hope this doesn't represent your literary critique," she said as the left side of her mouth rose to a grin.

"No. Just an unfortunate encounter with a wet dog."

"Ah—Franky. No wonder Matt's been calling me."

I nodded, the thought of Matt making me blush. "I have always enjoyed your writing. I just hope you have it saved on a disk somewhere. The message in your book is so important."

"It is, but telling my story is probably not the best way to share it. As you know, I'm not fond of exposure." She handed me back the book. "Any other confessions?" she asked.

"I broke the chair in the cottage. I promise to pay for it to be repaired."

"No need to worry about small things. It was an old chair."

"I'm really sorry, Emma."

"I'm sorry too." She said as she pulled me into a warm embrace— the kind of hug I had seen her give friends since I arrived in Aptos. Emma put her arm around my shoulders and we both looked up at the image of Mary. We sat in silence for several minutes before Emma looked down at her watch.

"It's almost dawn," She said. "Let's go see Camille. She loves to wake up early in the morning."

The early daylight shone through the window. The candles still flickered as we rose from the bench. Emma wrapped her arm around mine, and we walked down the hall. The hospital felt vacant. The still break of day brought crispness to the air and a smell that carried the scent of fresh tulips. We turned the corner past the reception area and saw Lynn sitting in a chair. Her broad shoulders were slumped with a curve. Her head rested in her clasped hands while a tear fell from the tip of her fingers. My chest filled with a sense of dread. Emma's eyes widened.

Lynn looked up at Emma. Her round, rosy cheeks drained to pale. She shook her head. "I'm sorry, Emma. Camille passed away a few minutes ago." Lynn reached for her hand. "She spoke to Jess, slept for a little bit, and then put this in my hand and asked me to give it to you."

Emma's face went stone white, her gaze recessing into her mind, not noticing the worn wood rosary beads Lynn placed in her hand.

"I swear, Emma, it was like she saw something she just had to go to. I am so sorry."

Emma stood motionless, breathless, and then swooned in my direction. Lynn jumped to her side, and we both held her as she slumped to the floor. Her eyes rolled up into her lids, closing for what felt like a lifetime before she came to. The silent language took over. We hovered into one another, squeezing each other tightly, weeping from a loss so deep it felt like it was coming from the core of the earth.

Chapter 12

Lynn pulled another bouquet of white tulips from the car and carried them into the courtyard. Two men in oversized T-shirts rolled wooden tables onto the patio and set them up with pink cotton cloths and white lattice-backed chairs. Emma told us that Camille wouldn't want her wake to be depressing, so we decorated it like a spring party. Florists and gardeners ran to make final touches to the yard while I sat at a table, folding cloth napkins, thinking about everything that had happened since the morning Camille died.

I called David that day to let him know that Emma was my aunt. I then told him about Camille and that I would be extending my trip. There was a long pause on the phone. We had been together so long that I could hear every thought in his labored sigh. He wondered how Emma would affect us; he sensed the distance in my voice and wasn't sure what to make of it. And he was ready to move on. Even for him, our relationship had grown stale. After we spoke, I sent my parents an e-mail. I didn't mention Emma or what I now knew about my birth mother, only that we needed to talk when I came home. I wanted to sit with my new reality and come to them in a clearer state of mind. After all, they were my parents and had given me a good life. Mostly, I didn't want to upset my father. He never let on much about his heart condition. But in the wake of Camille, I now felt that every day he was in my life was a precious one.

Jess arrived the day his mother passed away. He and Anna, the little girl he picked up for Oasis, were stuck living out of his truck for two days before passing over destroyed roads and immobile traffic to get to the eastern border of Arizona. Once across, they made their way home through the California desert and up through the San Joaquin Valley. They both stayed at Emma's house. Anna, with a toothless mouth she rarely exposed and a Hello Kitty barrette in her hair she wouldn't take off, slept on a cot at the foot of Emma's bed. Jess stayed in the room down the hall.

I watched Jess through the week as if I wanted to cover him for a story. He had light brown skin like Camille and her large oval eyes. His thick, dark hair waved back from his narrow forehead, and his lean body moved with the fluency of a lightweight boxer. The two of us were comfortable with each other from the beginning. We both helped with Anna and Emma, and the handoffs of responsibility between us needed little words as we quickly became part of the same team.

Anna and Emma were in fragile states. Jess tended to them with the loving presence of Camille and the strength of an eldest son suddenly called upon to fill his parent's shoes. As I watched him, stopping for long moments when he didn't think I was looking, seemingly captured by a blank stare, I wondered how he felt under his dutiful veneer. His heart was masked by a kind, sturdy face and an almost obsessive preoccupation with cooking.

Each morning, I would find Anna sitting on the counter, beating eggs under Jess's direction. I'd sit at the table with my coffee, waiting for Emma to come into the kitchen, as he taught Anna how to toss corn tortillas to land flat on the open flames. Anna would squeal every time one caught on fire, and Jess would quickly flip them in the air while her eyes remained fixed on his every motion. The steaming tortillas were placed on a plate, where he layered them with scrambled eggs and handfuls of tomatoes, green peppers, and onions before smothering the stack with white grated cheese.

Emma barely ate that week. She would come in for tea in the morning and then return to her room looking a little more energetic whenever Jess was near. After breakfast, Jess and Anna would go into town for the morning and return for an afternoon siesta. By early evening, he was back in the kitchen, baking bread, making chorizo, or chopping up meat for carne asada. He often had the cell phone to his ear while he cooked. Jess and Anna were now in daily contact with Anna's grandmother. Jess spoke to her in a cheerful Spanish the way I imagined he once spoke to his mother. When he hung up, he would often look at me, his eyes glassy with sadness that slowly lit to joy whenever he focused back on Anna.

That week was mostly spent sitting in silence with Emma and coloring on big pads of paper with Anna. She didn't speak a word of English when she arrived. By the end of the week, she had picked up a few dozen nouns and was putting together sentences. Emma said less than that. The candles stayed lit on the fireplace, and Emma's vigil for Camille had no end in sight. She wore her knit purple sweater every day of the week, and I suspected she slept in it, as if she were wearing Camille like a warm blanket. During the afternoons, I would catch her staring at the wall as if watching a movie. The left side of her mouth would rise in a smile and then fall moments later with a tear. She would look down and rub Camille's worn wood rosary beads, then close her eyes and breathe. The depth of her breath was so expansive, it was as if she was breathing in Camille's spirit in a way that was transforming her own.

The day before the funeral had been the most eventful. Emma's oldest son, Tai, had arrived from San Francisco. The air in the house seemed to change as soon as he reclaimed his bedroom from Jess and Jess moved into the cottage office until a plan could be finalized with Anna. Jess's fiancée, Maria, called or came by every hour that day. He would meet with her on the front porch, seeming concerned that her voice was too loud for the sensitive souls in the house. Before dinner, she stormed through the front door and demanded to see him.

Emma and I covered Anna's ears while we listened behind a closed door. She yelled at him for giving too much attention to everybody else in the house. Her words were followed by the clanging sound of her engagement ring being thrown against the kitchen cabinets. She then shouted what sounded like fast-paced profanity and stormed out of the house, clicking down the brick hall in heels that could aerate a lawn. We walked back into the kitchen. Jess just shook his head and started making guacamole.

I folded another napkin while the yard emptied of workers. Matt had been at the house several times that week to check in on Emma and Jess and had been there all morning, setting up the yard and helping where he could. It felt lighter when he was around. His mouth rested in a smile, and his clothes were often slightly disheveled, like he chose them from a pile on the floor.

We talked about his documentaries and the writer's life that I was now eager to return to. His friendship, along with Jess's, was making me feel like I was now part of the family.

"They will be here in about five minutes," Lynn yelled from the kitchen window.

"Okay, it's ready out here," I yelled back.

The funeral had ended over an hour ago, and Emma, Tai, and Jess had gone with the hearse to the cemetery for the burial. Over the week, Emma's face had taken on many hues, but that morning in church, when I watched her lean into Camille's casket and kiss her still body lightly on the forehead, Emma was at peace. Her shoulders relaxed as she walked back from the altar and joined us on the bench.

I felt Anna's hand weave around my small fingers as I folded the last napkin. A smile rose within me.

"Come," she said as she pulled me across the yard in the light green dress she picked out in the local children's store. "Come, come."

We walked around to the front of the porch, where Max lay with his long nose resting flat against the floor. His tail was limp.

His brown eyes were staring out over the driveway like an old man longing for his missing lover.

"Hey, Max. What's up, boy?" His tail slid a few inches across the floor. "Emma will be right back. I promise she's not going anywhere."

Anna rested her head against Max's fur and wrapped her arms around his back. "*Su madre llega a la casa. Muy pronto.*"

"*Si,*" I said, "*muy pronto.*"

We sat on the porch, petting the dog. Matt walked out of the house, and a car pulled into the turnabout. He tucked in his gray button-down shirt to flatten the wrinkles, and with a nervous breath, he asked me how he looked.

"*Muy guapo,*" I said.

He looked at Anna. "Is that good?" he asked.

Anna nodded as if she was trying to rock the bow out of her hair.

A group of people that looked like they might be Jess's friends stepped out of the car and walked up to the porch.

"Hi, Matt," said a blonde-haired woman as she walked toward us.

Anna lifted her head from the dog, squealed with excitement, and jumped into the woman's arms.

"How's my chica bonita?" the woman asked as she spun Anna around, her dress flaring out to the side, exposing her leather knee-high boots. Anna continued to squeal as if it were the only noise she could make, playing in the woman's long, sandy hair like she was being twirled by a mermaid.

"Hey, Jan," Matt said as he reached out and hugged her. He then opened his embrace and brought me into the circle. "Kate, this is Jan. She's a pediatrician at the children's hospital and one of the volunteers at Oasis."

"Oh ... you are the woman Jess has been taking her to see all week."

"One of them." She smiled and pushed her thick hair out of her eyes and behind her ear. "Anna here checked out just fine. She is a lucky little girl."

A lucky little girl. In the world of the Oasis workers, that meant she hadn't been raped or mutilated. At five years old, she was still a virgin, and what I had come to learn was that the majority of the children they picked up had been sexually abused. Many of them were victims of incest who were then sold into slavery because they were no longer pure.

Anna and Jan danced in the driveway when Max stood up and started to bark. His tail wagged while Sadie came tearing around the side yard. The dogs ran halfway down the gravel driveway to meet Emma's car. Jess drove the old Mercedes while Tai and Emma sat in the back.

The car stopped. Max sat next to the door, waiting for it to open, Tai, stepped out from the other side. He pulled on the lapels of the black suit that tailor-fit his lean body. His wet-looking black hair was combed off his forehead, and his face was as still and serious as it had been since the previous night when he arrived. Jess was his opposite in every way. He stepped out with an impish smile that spoke a thousand words of innocence, sadness, and a deep appreciation for a lifetime of being well loved. Jan walked up to him, holding Anna, now wiggling in her arms. She set Anna down, and Tai walked around the car to open Emma's door.

Emma rose from the car and stood tall in her black dress and long gray sweater. Strains of white hair fell loose around her face, the rest clipped behind her neck and falling down her back. Her complexion looked soft and moist, and the sturdy way she was standing made me think she was feeling stronger. Jess and Tai flanked her like bookends, escorting her up the stairs, with Max tailing behind, waiting to be noticed.

I walked up and kissed her on the check. Her lips rose, and she reached down and squeezed my hand.

"Are you okay?" I asked.

"I will be," she said. "Thank you for staying and for being here today."

"Of course."

Jan took a step toward Emma.

"I'm so glad you are here," Emma said to Jan, reaching out to hug her. "Camille thought the world of you."

"I think the world of her, too," Jan said as her eyes began to water. Anna's thumb rose to her mouth, and she rested her head on Jan's shoulder. Emma rubbed her back and kissed her on the head next to her Hello Kitty barrette.

"I hope the party is starting," Emma said in a tired voice. "Camille would not want us to be sitting around, crying."

"Then let's get it started!" Jess said, putting his arm around Emma.

Jack, the guy we met in San Francisco, arrived behind them and went in to tend the bar, wearing the same black jacket with sleeves too short to reach his wristwatch. He waited until the food was served and then mixed up a batch of elephant seals. Jess and Matt started the first round. Emma handed hers to Jan and opted for a glass of white wine.

"You want this?" Jan asked, offering me the drink.

"No, thank you. I've seen where that gets you."

She turned around and tossed the buttery rum concoction into the bushes. "How much longer are you here?" she asked.

"I'm leaving in the morning. I wish I could stay longer, but I need to get home to do a few things."

"Small-town gossip says you have a new aunt."

"That I do," I said, looking over at Emma smiling through her sadness as a group of people surrounded her. "Did you know Camille well?" I asked.

"I did. Jess and I dated in high school, and I've been one of the volunteers at Oasis since I was an intern." She touched the tip of Anna's nose. "She was a special lady."

"Yes, she was." I smiled at her and rubbed my fingers across Anna's hair. "That must have been fun dating Jess. He seems like a good guy."

"It was at the time. And now he is one of my very best friends."

"There you are," Lynn said to Jan as she walked up with an elephant seal in her hand. "I understand congratulations are in order."

"I hope so. Cross your fingers."

"Congratulations?"

"Jess and I are going to become Anna's legal parents."

"You don't have to be married to be her parents?"

"No. You both just have to agree to love her with all your heart," she said as she squeezed Anna into a wide, toothless smile that popped a dimple I hadn't seen. "She's going to start school next week, and the best news of all is that her grandmother has taken a job in Santa Cruz. They are going to be able to see each other as often as they like."

"Come on, ladies," Lynn said. "We don't want to leave Emma alone too long with Jack in the yard. God knows what he'll make for her to drink."

We walked through the white lattice arch and onto the patio. I had not been to too many funerals and even fewer wakes. But nothing compared to the feel of that day. White tulips were everywhere—in vases and wreaths, on tables and collared shirts, in planters throughout the garden and in arrangements that filled the house with the clean smell of nature's perfume. Every flower represented a child who was saved through the Oasis program. The sight of so many tulips and the thought that each was a child being educated instead of prostituted moved me to my core, a place where I was finding solid ground.

I looked across the yard and saw Anna still riding on Jess's back. Tai stood next to them with a drink in one hand while he loosened his taut black tie with the other. We had yet to find the words to connect. So far, a few awkward exchanges were the extent of our relationship. Hoping the drink had loosened him up a bit, I walked over to make another attempt.

"It was a beautiful ceremony," I said while he unbuttoned the collar of his shirt.

"I don't know if I would call it beautiful."

"What would you call it?"

"Necessary." He squinted into my eyes and then walked away.

"Don't mind him," Jan said, moving to my side. "He is probably the only person on earth that didn't like Camille."

"Why not?"

"Honestly, I think he was just jealous. Emma and Camille had something special, and I don't think Tai ever really understood it."

I watched Tai walk to the corner of the yard. "Were they lovers?" I asked.

"Nobody knows." She looked at me and smiled. "And it shouldn't matter to anybody but them."

I nodded and looked over at Emma, sitting at the top of a step to the garden. Anna had pulled the clip from her hair and was rubbing her fingers through her long gray strands.

"How do you think she's going to do without her?" I asked.

"I don't know. But I think it's no coincidence that Camille is the one that found you, and you were here when she passed over."

I thought of the first day when I met Camille in the flower shop. I was buying white tulips when she told me Emma Daines liked sunflowers. Now white tulips were everywhere. I could feel my mind stretch. There were so many little moments in life that were connected to other moments, to other people, to what seemed to be destined events, like a grand tapestry moving like specs in a kaleidoscope. Camille knew who I was all along. And perhaps on some level, she knew I would be standing here, watching over Emma, while she laid at rest in the cemetery up the hill.

Jan lifted up her water glass, and I cheered with my glass of wine. "To Camille," Jan said.

"To Camille," I echoed.

Jack walked up to us with a hurried pace, strains of thin hair falling onto his furrowed brow. "We need a quick Oasis meeting in the kitchen," he said to Jan before heading into the back door.

"Come on," she said.

I took Anna from her arms and followed her into the kitchen. Within a few minutes, Emma and Lynn walked in and stood by the counter. Behind them, Jess, Tai, and Matt pushed each other through the door.

"We have a bit of an urgent situation," Jack said as he lifted his cell phone to show us a picture of a little brown-skinned girl, her long hair in a braid and a big smile on her face that revealed a small space in her mouth where her first baby tooth had fallen. "We need to pick this little girl up as soon as possible. Her name is Somsri. She is the younger sister of the child I picked up last week. The traders were so angry that we got there before them that they are now threatening the family. This little girl is at serious risk."

"How soon do we need to get her?" Emma asked.

"In the next forty-eight hours."

"You know the area. Why don't you go?" asked Tai.

"I can't. I have to cover Camille's presentation to the Gates funding committee on Monday. It could mean millions of dollars to Oasis."

"I can't leave Anna right now," Jess said before looking over to Lynn as the next likely choice.

"I'll go."

The room turned so quiet, it was as if everybody had stopped breathing.

"I'll take the first flight out tomorrow," I said with a steadiness in my voice I didn't recognize. They all just looked at me.

"Are you sure you want to do that?" Lynn asked.

"It could be dangerous," Jack said, "especially under these conditions."

"That's okay. I can do it," I said. "I want to go get her."

Emma looked at me but remained quiet. She nodded several times, her sturdy gaze communicating her support.

"Okay," Jake said. "I'll get you what you will need in the morning." He looked around the room at astonished eyes. "Meeting adjourned. Let's go get a drink."

The group dispersed. Tai walked out of the room while Matt, Jan, and Jess came up and hugged me.

"I can try and move some things and go with you," Matt said.

"No, that's okay. I think this is something I need to do on my own."

Emma and Lynn stood looking at each other and then back at me.

Lynn opened her arms, inviting me into them. "You are definitely related to Emma," she said. Emma came up and rubbed my back. "Actually, today I think you are more related to Camille."

Jess and Matt walked into the back rooms and returned with guitars. "Fire pit time," Jess said as they scooted out the back door. Jan, Emma, and Lynn followed them out. I stood there for a moment, not wanting to move. Everything inside of me felt solid, as if I had just come into alignment with my purpose. I clasped my hands and started to rub my small fingers. They felt softer, not as tight against the bigger fingers or as curled into my palm.

"The boys are waiting on you," Emma said, popping her head through the kitchen door.

"I'll be right there."

The round dining tables had been moved to the side, and chairs were set around a fire pit on the patio. In the pit was a stack of wood that Jack lit with the juice from an elephant seal. The next few hours were filled with songs, toasts to Camille, memories shared, and stories that made us laugh in unison and shed tears of collective sadness. The sorrow was edging up against something sweet. We were all there out of love for one amazing woman who, in life and death, was connecting our hearts to each other in a way that made the group stronger than any one individual. In that moment, sitting by the fire, bound by a common love, I felt the true gift of Camille as a piece of her spirit entered my own.

Jess put down his guitar and took Anna from Jan. Her heavy lids fell closed while he cradled her in his arms. Matt then looked at me and caught my eyes. Pushing up his sleeves, exposing his buffalo tattoo, he lifted the guitar under his arm and started to play. The picking vibration of the strings harmonized with his voice.

Blackbird singing in the dead of night,
Take these broken wings and learn to fly.
All your life,
You were only waiting for this moment to arise.
Blackbird, fly
Into the light of the dark black night.

He looked over at me as he played. Through each chorus, I felt thankfully seen and strangely reassured. It was time to fly. And I was flying into the light of the dark, black night to Thailand.

The crowd began to leave just after midnight. Tai and Jan drove a few of the guests home while Jess took Anna into the house and tucked her into bed. Lynn and I were washing dishes in the kitchen, and Emma remained in the yard, sitting in an Adirondack chair, wrapped in a dark-gray lap blanket, facing the crackling fire rising from the open pit. The dogs lay on either side of her chair, looking as reflective as she did.

"So what did you decide to do about your marriage situation?" Lynn asked as she reached for a wet plate to dry.

"I decided that if I haven't married him by now, there is probably a reason for that."

"Did you tell him?"

"I didn't have to. He moved out this weekend. He called me yesterday and told me when I was ready to get married to call him. And if he was still available, he would consider it."

"And how did that make you feel?"

"Liberated. I don't think I realized how much I was trying to please him and my father."

She nodded. "I guess that made your decision to go to Thailand easier."

"It wouldn't have mattered. Either way, I would have volunteered to go. It was the right decision for me."

"Good for you. It sounds like you have overcome your own obstacle course."

"For now, but I'm sure there will be another one."

"There always is." Lynn said as she looked out the window and then threw me the drying towel. "Your aunt looks like she could use a little company right now."

I peeked out the window at Emma in her chair, then heated the teapot and put together a tray of mint leaves and chocolate-dipped biscotti that had become our nightly routine. Lynn and I said good night, and I walked out to the yard and handed Emma her cup. She smiled and reached for my hand.

"Sit down," she said.

I sat down in a chair across from her. The flickering glow cast a shadow on Emma's face. The lines in her forehead that were so pronounced through the week had vanished. Her shoulders were at rest in the chair, her skin as smooth as an early-morning sea. She exhaled deeply and took a sip of tea. "So you are going to Thailand."

"I don't think I could have said no. My heart was pulling on me to volunteer as soon as he said there was a child at risk."

"That is how it works," she said.

"Is that an invitation?"

She smiled as if amused that I had remembered. "I think your invitation came when you lost your job and you decided to take the opportunity to allow yourself to grow. Now, my dear, I think you are going on your journey."

Her words struck me as truth. I felt like I was about to leave on a mission, and much like my trip to Aptos, I knew I would not come back the same. "What about you?" I asked.

"What about me?" she said, reflecting on the question. "I'm really not sure what this is asking of me. But I've done this long enough to know that it is asking something." She looked down at her tea. "All I know right now is that I'm sure going to miss her."

"I'm sorry."

"There is nothing to be sorry about. It's just life. Always unpredictable."

The kitchen door opened, and Jess walked toward us in his black down jacket. He placed a blanket around my shoulders. "Anna is asleep," he said. "Do you mind checking in on her before you go to bed?"

"I'd love to. Where are you going?" Emma asked.

"I thought I would head down to Mom's house for the night. I need some time with her," he said as he looked into the fire.

"I'll leave my door open so I can hear Anna. You take your time, Jess."

"Thanks," he said as he bent down and kissed Emma on the top of the head. "See you both in the morning."

We wished him good night and focused back on the fire. The stacks of wood had burned into pieces. The flames had shortened their spikes while the embers radiated a heat so warm I had to open the blanket around my shoulders to cool down. Emma wrapped her hands around her teacup and rested her soft gaze on mine.

"I've been thinking about you," she said. "When you come back from Thailand, I'd like to sit down and discuss a few things."

"About the articles you want written?"

"About what happened to Sarah. It's probably time I let that go too, and I want to give you the interview."

I looked at her as my heart warmed. Everything I wanted when I first came to Aptos, I realized I didn't want now. Her story was her life, her history; it was part of what made her Emma. There wasn't a cell in my body that wanted to sell that for gain.

"Thank you. But I can't take your story. It's sacred, Emma. It belongs with you and only with you."

"But Kate, you can use it to get a fine job. I can call a friend at the *Times* and another at the *New Yorker*. In those publications, you can write the kind of meaningful stories you like to write."

"Again, thank you for such a kind offer, but I think there is a more meaningful story for me here."

"Here?"

"Yes. I've been talking with Jess, and if you don't mind, when I come back from Thailand, I'd like to help out with Oasis. I want to help keep Camille's mission alive, and I'd like to help you find the audience for your message. I believe in what you're doing, and I feel it, too. The world is going through something right now, and people need help managing the changes. I want to be part of that message."

Emma smiled—not just from the right side of her mouth, but for a moment, the left side slightly rose too. "Are you sure?" she asked.

"Positive."

Soft pleats of skin formed around Emma's eyes. She shook her head in disbelief and then let out a loud sigh. "Nothing would make me happier," she said.

The broken logs fell to embers, and the night became still. We both looked up at the sky. The stars had brightened to a tapestry of white tulips that twinkled the reminder that they were the constant, and the drama of life was simply an invitation to help us ascend toward the heavens.

Please join the Emma Daines Sociey at DawnKohler. com to receive book updates, enjoy character and plot discussions, and receive helpful tips on how you, like the characters, can best manage the changes in your life to align yourself with a greater sense of purpose and giving.

Made in the USA
San Bernardino, CA
29 October 2014